CUCKOO CUCKOO

CUCKOO
CUCKOO

NICHOLAS PONTICELLO

BOOLEANOP, LOS ANGELES, CALIFORNIA

To Dr. Casalegno—for helping me make sense of my own crazy family.

FOREWORD

THE YEAR WAS 2015, and Donald Trump was running for president. I wouldn't be born for another eight years—on October 11, 2023—thanks to the last living will and testament of my donor, Mr. Charles B Vanderough. You see, the last living will and testament of Charles B Vanderough stipulated that I be fashioned precisely one year after his death. And so I was. I am Charles B Vanderough's clone.

This next part gets tricky. Charles B Vanderough was also a clone. He was fashioned after Mr. Charles Abernathy Vanderough. Charles Abernathy Vanderough was the original. So that makes me the clone of a clone.

Henceforth, I shall refer to myself as Charlie C.

My donor, Charlie B, was fashioned on June 16, 1997. He was only twenty-five years old when he died. No doubt you read all about it in *Scientific American* and the *New York Times*. Contrary to what the papers said at the time, Charlie B did not die of medical complications resulting from the cloning process. He merely jumped off a bridge.

And Charles Abernathy Vanderough, Charlie B's donor, was fashioned the ordinary way—from the random collision of a spermatozoon with an egg—on February 7, 1962. He was thirty-four years old when he died from a bullet to his brain. Incidentally, he was the one who put the bullet in his brain.

I am currently forty-seven years old, so I have already outlived both of my predecessors by more than a decade. Not that I haven't come close to dying. I recently overdosed on prescription opioids and am now under the doctors' care at the Green Slopes Psychiatric Hospital in Overton, Vermont.

It is from this clean, white room with a window overlooking a big green lawn that I now write the story of Charlie B.

—CCV

CHAPTER 1

O N JUNE 16, 2015, Charlie B turned eighteen. He was sitting for his exit exams in Dean Cudgel's office when Tiger B skidded by and hissed, "Donald Trump is running for president!"

Dean Cudgel was dozing in the chair behind his desk. Charlie B looked up from his exam booklet.

"What does Donny B have to say about that?" Charlie asked in a whisper.

"He says he knows better than to ever run for president."

The two boys chuckled. Dean Cudgel snorted, and Tiger ran off to share the news with the rest of the boys at Price-Harold.

Price-Harold had been Charlie B's only home for as far back as he could remember. The big stately manor and its dormitories had once been a Protestant church in the early nineteenth century. After a fire in 1837, the building stood abandoned and in disrepair for nearly one hundred years until a wealthy textile baron named Jerimiah Smith secured the deed to the estate. Smith founded the Price-Harold School for Boys in 1934. But it wasn't until 1997, a year after Dolly the sheep became the first mammal to be cloned, that Price-Harold admitted its first human clone, Warren B—then only an infant—to be raised exclusively at Price-Harold.

The school had become a home to clones ever since, specializing in a first-class education in art and science. None of this was public knowledge, of course. The few wealthy donors whose clones were brought up at Price-Harold expected total privacy. To the outside world, Price-Harold was merely a boarding school for ne'er-do-well boys whose parents had shipped them off for a disciplined education.

Charlie B was in the same year as Warren B. There were only twelve clones graduating in 2015—Warren B had been the first to go. Then William B had graduated in March. Fahd B had gone last April. And now that Charlie B was eighteen years old, he needed only to pass his exit exams to be set free.

Charlie B filled in the last bubble in the exam booklet and put his pencil down. Dean Cudgel was still dozing in his chair.

"Ahem." Charlie coughed.

Dean Cudgel sat upright and blinked blearily about the room. "Done, my boy?"

"Yes, sir."

"Very well. Run upstairs to pack. I'll have it graded before noon."

"Yes, sir."

Charlie had already packed, so he went up to his room to wait. He was sitting on his naked mattress when Headmistress Fruth appeared in the doorway.

"Charlie B," she said.

"Yes, ma'am." Charlie jumped up.

"I've come to congratulate you personally on passing your exams."

"Thank you, ma'am."

Headmistress Fruth looked about the empty room. "I see you're all ready to go."

"Yes, ma'am."

Headmistress Fruth nodded. Then she produced a large manila envelope and handed it to Charlie. "I suggest you read through your file carefully. Willie will call you a car when you're ready. It will take you wherever you want to go."

"Yes, ma'am."

Headmistress Fruth stuck out her hand. Charlie shook it.

"Good luck, Charlie B."

CHAPTER 2

BRIAN GLAZIER sat at his office desk scrolling through YouTube footage of police shootings. He had been busy overseeing a major remodel of his kitchen and had missed the news about Freddie Gray's death from injuries sustained in the back of a police van on April 12, 2015.

"I don't get it," Brian Glazier mumbled to his office mate, Grayson McDougal. "Our boys in blue are just trying to do their jobs. It's dangerous out there for a cop these days."

Grayson was flipping through the top-ten botched nose jobs of 2014 online when he saw a pop-up window announcing Donald Trump's bid for the Republican ticket.

"Donald Trump is running for president," Grayson declared.

"Finally," Brian said. "A man who can actually get something done. Not one of those paid-off politicians in Washington. Now here's someone who can finally fix this mess."

CHAPTER 3

CHARLIE WAS IN HIS ROOM staring at the unopened envelope when Eric B came in.

"Donald Trump is running for president," Eric said.

"I heard," Charlie replied.

Eric crossed the room and plopped down on Charlie's bare mattress.

"I can't believe you're leaving," he said. "Couldn't you have, you know, failed your exams—like Shau-kee B? He gets to stick around another year. I'm thinking that isn't such a bad idea now that *my* birthday is around the corner."

"I'm ready to get out of here," Charlie said. Then he nodded to the manila envelope on his desk.

"Is that—it?" Eric asked. "It looks so—"

"Small? Yeah, that's what I thought when Fruth handed it to me."

"Have you...?"

Charlie shook his head, indicating the unbroken seal on the envelope. "I want to wait until I'm out of this dungeon."

"Where are you going to go?"

"I suppose I'll head into the city."

The cuckoo clock in the hall chimed the quarter hour.

"I'm going to be late for practice," Eric said. "You'll write and let me know when you've settled down somewhere?"

"Yes, I'll write."

Eric grasped Charlie's hand and pulled him in for a quick hug. Then he was out the door.

Charlie watched from the third-story window as Eric joined several other boys heading for the clubhouse. When the cuckoo clock chimed again, Charlie zipped up his leather duffel bag, stuffed the manila envelope under his arm, and headed out the door.

CHAPTER 4

BRIAN GLAZIER pulled the 2015 GMC Yukon up the long roundabout and into the shelter of the four-car garage. His wife's 2015 Mercedes-Benz GLA-Class sat parked next to the 1970 Chevrolet Monte Carlo.

"Terri must have finished up at Bunco early," Brian said to no one in particular.

Sam was playing ball in the driveway, taking half-court shots at the hoop over the garage. Beyond him, Brian could see Terri and Adele playing in the kiddy pool. It was hot in Silicon Valley, hotter than Brian remembered it being in years. The weatherman had said something about six of the ten hottest years on record occurring in the past decade.

"Climate change," the weatherman had indicated.

"Total crap," Brian had muttered to himself as he had taken the off-ramp for Menlo Park. *What about the ice age? What about when the planet was a molten ball of lava?*

"Honey," Terri called out as Brian traversed the drive. "The chicken should be about done. Can you turn off the oven? I'm watching Adele in the pool."

Inside, Brian flipped the switch on their new GI-82 convection oven.

Adele came running into the kitchen with a towel wrapped around her head. She bolted for the bedroom. Terri followed, calling, "Don't get water all over the house."

"She just tracked grass all over the new carpet," Brian muttered, checking the temperature gauge on the chicken.

"Yolanda is coming tomorrow," Terri said. "She'll take care of it."

"Last time, she didn't even get those rings out of the sink. I think we should start thinking about looking for somebody more professional," Brian complained. "Plus, I don't love that she brings her kids out here during the summer. Can't she put them in summer camp like everybody else?"

"I'll ask her." Terri started dressing the salad. Music played over the home stereo system. Terri hummed along. Brian checked on the potatoes and then called Sam in from outside.

After some time, Terri continued, "What's the deal with Adele? Not our Adele. The singer Adele. Wasn't she supposed to release another album, like, ages ago?"

"Mike over at streaming tells me it will be out by November. I guess they're trying to negotiate a deal for the new streaming platform."

"Adele!" Adele squealed, coming in from the bedroom in her bathrobe.

"Yes, honey," Terri said. "I promise we'll get you front-row tickets the minute she goes on tour."

CHAPTER 5

WILLIE JACKSON was in his usual spot, with his chair tipped back and his feet up on the heavy wooden desk that served as a security checkpoint for visitors.

"Mister Charles!" he said cheerfully as Charlie B approached. "Graduation day already?"

"Yes, Willie," Charlie said. "I'm outta here."

"I'll call you a car," Willie said, the whites of his eyes shining brightly against the dark brown and ruddy red of his acne-scarred cheeks. Willie disappeared into a side office to use the phone. He reappeared moments later, beaming.

"I remember when you were a baby, Mister Charles," Willie said. "I sat you on this desk and played peekaboo with you for hours."

"You never told me that, Willie."

"Hmph! I haven't told you half of what I know," Willie retorted, his once-chipper face sinking into a scowl. "People like me aren't allowed to tell what they know."

"What's that supposed to mean?"

The students at Price-Harold were accustomed to Willie's moody episodes. Charlie should have known better than to ask questions.

"What I mean is Freddie Gray," Willie retorted. "And all those other kids getting shot up all over the place. It's a damn shame."

"It is," Charlie said. "I agree."

"So what're you gonna do about it?" Willie rejoined. "Now you're free to do as you please, what are *you* gonna do about this great big American shame of ours?"

"I don't know what you mean, Willie."

"Look at yourself," he replied. "A white boy. The educated clone of a rich, rich man. You can do anything you want. Now how many of the boys here are Black? Tell me that? How many of the boys at this school are as Black as I am?"

"There's Tiger B—"

"OK, Tiger B. Who else?"

Charlie B thought for a long time. It was true. There were Chinese, Korean, and Japanese students. There were several Latino kids as well. But except for Tiger B, Charlie had never seen another Black student at Price-Harold.

"That's right," Willie spouted. "There aren't any others. There never were. That is what we call *institutionalized racism.*"

Charlie was growing weary of Willie's tirade—he found

himself glancing furtively out the window to see if the car had arrived.

Willie must have seen his face, because he suddenly settled down into his usual state of repose and said, "Now look how I've gotten myself all worked up. These young men getting killed all over the country is a damn shame. But it's no reason to spoil your graduation day, Mister Charles. I'll check on that car."

Willie disappeared into the little side office. When he came back, he was grinning ear to ear and clasping something tight in his left hand.

"I got you a little going-away gift," he said, plopping a black circular pin into Charlie's palm. On it, in block lettering, were the words "black lives matter."

"If more folks take a stand," Willie said proudly, "then maybe we'll see a difference. Yes, siree. Mister Charles, you *can* make a difference."

Charlie shifted the shiny black pin in the palm of his hand, trying to imagine what in the world Willie meant by the strange parting gift.

"Now look at that, Mister Charles," Willie resumed. "Your car is here."

Willie walked Charlie out to the waiting car and opened the passenger door.

"Good luck, Mister Charles."

And with that, Willie closed the door of the black sedan and disappeared inside the school.

CHAPTER 6

CHARLIE DITCHED the Black Lives Matter button in the back of the town car. The whole ride to the train depot, he'd been thinking about what Willie had said to him about being the clone of a "rich, rich man."

All the boys at Price-Harold were worth their weight in gold. But there was a difference between being rich and being *rich* rich. And up until then, Charlie had always assumed he was merely rich. Vanderough was not a household name like Trump or Woods. Wikipedia described Charles Abernathy Vanderough as an eccentric recluse who dabbled in venture capital and horse racing. Google searches never turned up anything more than his cryptic obituary, which read as follows:

> Charles Abernathy Vanderough. Died September 8, 1996. He suffered from a series of complications. And he is survived by a series of complications.

So Charlie knew very little about the man—and how much he was worth. Donny B was lucky; his donor was splattered across every paper and news site around the world, whereas Charlie's donor was a complete mystery.

The town car had taken Charlie as far as Penn Station. He'd slept on and off during the commute, trying desperately to ignore the driver, who wanted to talk about his upcoming vacation plans to Fiji. Charlie hadn't wanted to open his file in front of the driver, so he'd clutched it in his hands all the way to the train depot.

Charlie had about $200 in spending money—his monthly allowance from Headmistress Fruth. The driver continued to bore Charlie with details about his personal life as he unloaded the leather duffel from the trunk. Charlie tipped him $50. He always tipped big. Then he found a Dunkin' Donuts, ordered an egg sandwich and a cup of black coffee, and retreated to a quiet corner of the train station with his file.

He unsealed the flap of the manila envelope gently with his thumb and removed a stack of papers about a quarter-inch thick. The first twenty pages were school records—transcripts, a copy of his diploma, and other paraphernalia from Price-Harold. Then he discovered a phony birth certificate and a social security card. He'd never seen either of these things before, so he stared at them a good long while, savoring the little details—like the made-up names of his mother and father, Beatrice and Wilbur Vanderough—that tethered him to the land of the living.

There was a fresh new debit card with pin number 0240. Charlie looked around for an ATM.

Then he saw the letter. Handwritten. A loose scrawl. Custom stationery with gilded margins and the words "Helmsley Park" emblazoned on the header.

The letter was dated August 15, 1996.

Dear Charles B,

I am told that this letter will not reach you until your eighteenth birthday. That puts us somewhere in the twenty-first century. I will be long dead by then. I hesitate to offer any words of advice except these: you must make an honest living for yourself. Your life depends on it.

I have been miserable my whole life because everything came too easily to me. My grandmother on my mother's side came into money when her father struck gold in California in 1849. My father came into money when his father struck oil in Texas in 1908. And I came into money when my father died.

None of us were happy people. Not for any sustained period of time, anyway. You should know that you come from a long line of depressives. And who's to blame? No doubt our DNA has as much to do with it as anything. But that cannot be all. Much of my misery, I assure you, comes from idleness borne from too much wealth and privilege too early in life.

So I will spare you that fate. I leave you a total of $45,000, which shall be kept in a high-yield checking account on your behalf until you are old enough to claim the sum for yourself. At which time, you are to do as I say—or else wind up the unhappiest of men.

First, you must put a roof over your head. It is no use to anyone you sleeping on the street. I have allotted $12,000 for rooming expenses. You must find an affordable place to live at approximately $1,000 a month. That will give you a solid year to get on your feet.

Next, you are to furnish the apartment with the most basic necessities: a bed, a desk, and a library of good books. For this purpose, I give you $4,000.

Once you have settled the living arrangements to your satisfaction, you must purchase two nice suits. They needn't be too nice. The suits are to be worn to job interviews, so their quality need only demonstrate to future employers that you are a sensible and gentlemanly sort of person. For the suits, I have set aside $1,800.

Then you must find a job. You have about one year before your allowance runs out. I have provided $600 a month for provisions, travel costs, and other minor expenses ($7,200). Once a job is secured, you will begin earning your own money, and you needn't fear running out of your inheritance any more than you fear running out of air to breathe. Like the plants on God's green earth, you will be making your own air, so to speak.

Lastly, I have set aside $20,000 for schooling. I encourage you to enroll immediately in any one of the local colleges. City colleges are particularly affordable and accommodating to part-time students with jobs. You must educate yourself if you are to make an honest living. I never did, and I have regretted it every day of my pitiful life.

You can work days and take classes at night. And within a year, you should find yourself the happiest man on the planet.

Good luck and God bless.
Charles Abernathy Vanderough

Charlie threw down the letter in disbelief. Then he stuck the debit card into the nearest ATM and punched in the pin. The balance read $45,425.74.

From as far back as Charlie could remember, he'd been told that he would have it made when he got out of Price-Harold. He was the clone of one of the wealthiest men in the country. He was destined for a life of greatness. Picture this: A villa in the Adirondacks. A stock portfolio totaling in the hundreds of millions. Butlers, maids, footmen, oh my!

And what was he really worth?

A measly forty-five grand.

A train whistled in the station.

Charlie withdrew $600 for incidentals, shoved the cash into his pocket, and then winced seeing the balance on the account drop to $44,825.74. Charles Abernathy Vanderough had cheated him out of his rightful inheritance. And furthermore, the letter provided no additional insight into Charlie's ancestry, his family, and his true origin. *Beatrice and Wilbur Vanderough!* What a crock of shit. He was an orphan with a meager pittance. A penniless pauper.

And then Charlie remembered: the stationery. He fumbled through the manila envelope and withdrew the handwritten letter from the file. There it was, on the footer of the page— the address for Helmsley Park.

* * *

Charlie caught the overnight train to Holyoke, Massachusetts. From there, he would catch a bus to Amherst. Then it was just a quick cab ride out to the old Vanderough estate. Charlie had decided to try his luck there. Surely some relative or another would take pity on him.

Charlie paid the premium price for a sleeper car: $355. He lay awake listening to the *thump-thump* of the rails. Sometime around midnight, the train pulled into the New Haven station. Another six hours to Holyoke.

I could just hop off now and go back to my old life, Charlie thought. *Beg Headmistress Fruth to let me stay on for one more year. Buy some time while I figure out my next step.*

No. Charlie would go on to Helmsley Park. Scope things out. Play nice with Mrs. Charles Vanderough or Charles Junior or whomever still lived at the estate. Surely the Vander-ough fortune had gone to one or another of his relatives. And surely there was enough of it to go around.

Charlie slept a few hours on the train. The conductor's cry woke him at 5:00 a.m. They were an hour out from Holyoke. Breakfast was served in the dining car. Charlie ate his fill of whole-wheat pancakes and fried potatoes and tipped the waiter forty dollars.

CHAPTER 7

"**G**OOD MORNING, BOSTON!**" said Caroline Shore, a twentysomething news anchor for HBC's morning show, *Wake Up, Boston!*

"And good morning, Caroline," said cohost Ted Gumbel. "Sounds like you had an extra shot of espresso this morning."

"You know it, Ted," Caroline replied.

"What's with the espresso maker, by the way?" interjected a third cohost—Raquel Vasquez. "This morning I couldn't get the thing to start."

"Did you try the on button?" Ted rejoined.

All three broke out in laughter.

"No, but seriously," Caroline cut in. "I'm sure you've all heard the news already. Donald Trump is running for president."

"Oh, I loved the *Apprentice*," Raquel blurted.

"You're fired!" shouted Ted.

All three burst into a fit of laughter again.

"I don't know about this guy," Ted continued. "I mean, is he serious?"

"You know," Raquel said, "I met him once at a party. And when he walked in, it was like—I can't explain it. It was like this energy filled the room. It was, like, all unicorns and rainbows."

"Donald Trump was all unicorns and rainbows?"

"No, seriously, guys," Raquel went on. "I think he's got something special."

"Let's see what the audience thinks. Tweet us with your thoughts and then go to our website to see what others are saying."

"In other news, heat waves in parts of California yesterday killed eight people. The victims were said to be elderly residents in rural parts of the state."

"I'm actually freezing here in the studio." Ted interrupted.

"Yeah, it's like Alaska in here," said Raquel. "Can't we funnel some of this cold air out to California?"

"Brr."

"Up next, how to pull off the perfect barbeque this Fourth of July…"

CHAPTER 8

THE CAB DRIVER let Charlie out at the end of a long drive. A high stone wall surrounded the estate. The gatehouse was empty. Charlie shimmied through a gap in the wrought iron fence and proceeded up the drive.

Helmsley House was huge. It had to have at least a dozen private rooms. It was a Queen Anne Victorian manor, circa 1880, with a cross-gabled gray slate roof. Parapeted dormer windows protruded from the second and third stories, their steep gables interlaced with intricate stone cross-hatching. A cantilevered polygonal tower extended from the second story and climbed two and a half stories to the top of the house. Cutaway bay windows decorated with patterned masonry added to the deliberate asymmetry of the façade. An ornate porch wrapped around the north and east sides of the manor, topped by a partial front-facing porch over the entryway. Bands of green-slate-stone detailing separated the first and second floors, and the north face of the house boasted at least two dozen white sash Palladian and cottage windows.

The manor at Helmsley Park had to be one of the largest Queen Anne houses in the state—perhaps in the country. A house like this was easily worth several million.

The paved drive curved up to the carriage house, slicing a clean path through a sloping green lawn dotted with hemlocks and junipers. Two large ash trees stood on either side of the manor. The lawn stretched out in all directions for at least half a mile and abutted a planted cedar grove that grew from east to west in perfect alignment with the spindly white balustrades on the first-story porch.

It was early yet. Perhaps eight o'clock in the morning. There were no signs of movement around the house.

Charlie made his way up the drive and climbed the six stairs leading to the large oak doors. Green and red ivy clung to the walls on this side of the house. The sound of a radio issued from one of the upstairs bedrooms.

Charlie rang the bell.

There was the muffled sound of slippers on wooden stairs. Then the doors swung wide open.

"Mm, yeah?" It was a kid, maybe fourteen years old, sporting SpongeBob boxers and a loose white T-shirt. He was looking down at an iPhone while he spoke.

"Hello," Charlie said. "Are your parents home?"

"Mm, let me check." He shuffled back inside, still staring at his phone. "Mom! It's for you."

The volume on the radio upstairs went up. It was an early-morning talk program. The host was arguing with a medical expert about the necessity of early-childhood inoculations.

The kid loitered in the foyer, texting away on his phone. Charlie lingered on the porch, listening to the program on the radio.

"I have a friend whose daughter was perfectly fine before she went in for her vaccinations," the radio host said. "A beautiful little girl. No health problems at all. And the next thing you know, she's diagnosed with Asperger's syndrome. How do you explain that?"

The medical expert began citing facts from a recent study.

"Coming!" cried a voice from upstairs.

"She's coming," the kid said. Then he shuffled down the hall and disappeared around a corner.

The volume on the radio went up another notch.

"And what about in countries where they don't have vaccines?" the host continued. "They have a whole lot less autism there than we have here. Autism is on the rise in this country. What is that about?"

A woman appeared at the top of the landing, her graying hair in curlers.

"Who in God's name—?" she was muttering as she tromped down the stairs.

Then she saw Charlie and froze.

"Ron!" she called back up the stairs. "Ron! You'd better come see this."

"Hello," Charlie ventured. "Mrs. Vanderough?"

"Ronald!" she cried, her voice rising in pitch. "Get down here!"

"What is it, Maggie?" came a deeper voice.

Then a stout man appeared on the landing. He was straightening his tie.

"Oh my God!" he said when he saw Charlie. Then the man's feet slipped out from under him, and he tumbled down the last flight of stairs.

"Ron!" the woman screamed.

Charlie jumped inside the door and crouched over the shaken man.

"Are you OK?"

"Get away from me!" he cried. "Back! Back!"

Charlie slowly retreated.

"Maggie!" he bellowed.

Maggie came trundling down the stairs.

"Oh my God," she said, stooping to Ron's side. "Are you hurt? Talk to me, Ron!"

"Mmmph," said Ron, looking frazzled.

"Ethan!" she called over her shoulder. "Your father's hurt. Call an ambulance!"

"What?" came the boy's voice from somewhere deep inside the house.

"No. No," Ron said. "I don't need an ambulance. Just bruised my ass. That's all."

Then he looked up from his seat on the floor. Maggie's

gaze followed his, and they both stared at Charlie B.

"Who the hell are you?" Ron demanded.

Charlie shifted on his feet. Part of him wanted to run. Head for the hills.

"My name is Charles Vanderough."

"No, it's not," Ron said. "Charles Vanderough was my brother. And he died a long time ago."

"I'm also Charles Vanderough—" Charlie began to explain.

"Oh God!" Maggie cried. "You're his son! He *did* have an affair! I knew it."

Ron muttered, "The spitting image—"

"No," Charlie interjected. "I'm not his son. I'm his clone."

Ron fell back onto the floor. Maggie screeched and sat squarely on her rump beside him.

"What in God's name?"

"He made a clone?"

Just then Ethan shuffled in. "Mom, do we have any more milk. Hey, what's wrong?"

"What's wrong is that I'm still standing out here on the porch," Charlie said, "while your parents squirm around on the floor."

"Excuse me?" blurted Ron, sitting up indignantly.

"I was taught to invite my guests into the parlor and offer them something to drink," Charlie announced. He couldn't think of anything else to say. But as the two figures wriggling on the floor couldn't seem to pull themselves together, Charlie felt he had no other choice than to be firm and lean on his good breeding.

"Mom?" Ethan stammered.

"Yes, yes," she said, straightening up. "Get our guest something to drink. What would you like to drink, um, Mister—?"

"Charlie. I go by Charlie."

"Charlie," she said, standing. Then she nudged Ron with her foot. He stood.

"Very well," Ron said. "Come in. Let me show you to the *parlor*."

"I'd like a brandy, if you please," Charlie said, still assuming the air of superiority that he had decided was appropriate for these country bumpkins.

"He'd like a brandy," barked Ron.

"I don't know where you guys keep the brandy," Ethan complained.

"Like hell you don't!"

"Ron," Maggie interrupted. "I'll get Mister, um, Charlie some brandy. Why don't you offer him a chair?"

They had moved into the large, ornate living room. The furniture looked as if it hadn't been used in decades.

"Sit down," Ron said. "Maggie is going to get you some brandy. Ethan, stop staring. Go get ready for school."

"Dad, what's going on?"

"This here is *Charles Vanderough*," Ron said. "Your uncle's clone."

"What?" Ethan looked up from his phone for the first time since Charlie had arrived. "Holy shit."

"Watch your language, you little mongrel," Ron barked. "Mr. Vanderough is a refined gentleman."

Charlie was glad to be recognized for what he was: a gentleman. He softened a little.

"Charlie," he said. "Please call me Charlie."

Ron continued. "Now Charlie here and I are going to catch up, see. And you'll go straight to school and not say a word about this to anyone."

"Too late," Ethan said, already typing away on his iPhone.

"You little shit!" Ron barked.

Ethan shuffled out of the room to the sound of his fingers tapping away on the little screen.

At precisely that moment, the cuckoo clock on the parlor wall chimed the quarter hour. It was a Black Forest chalet clock with a little mahogany cuckoo bird and Biergarten dancers, just like the one outside Charlie's dorm room at Price-Harold.

"So, um, how do you do?" Ron asked, assuming a more formal tone.

"I'm well, thank you," Charlie said. "I'm sorry to call at such an early hour. I can come back later if you prefer."

"Oh no. You're not going anywhere!" Ron said, reassuming his brusque manner. "Not until we figure out what the hell is going on."

"Whatever you prefer," Charlie said, feigning politeness.

"Damn right!"

Ron stood up and paced back and forth along the edge of a Victorian needlepoint rug.

"You're the spitting image of him, you know? From when we were kids. You gotta be, what? Seventeen? Eighteen?"

"Eighteen."

"You look just like him when he was eighteen."

"Do you have any pictures?" Charlie asked. "I've never seen a photograph of Mr. Vanderough."

"Maggie will know where the pictures are. But you needn't bother. You're a perfect replica."

"Clone," Charlie said. "We prefer to be called clones."

"Fine. You're a perfect clone."

Maggie came in with the brandy and perched herself on a carved mahogany settee upholstered in blue velvet and embroidered with fleurs-de-lis. Charlie was sitting in a contemporary upholstered club chair, done over in red foliated cotton.

"Ron, dear," she said. "I was thinking—"

"You've given me and Maggie quite a shock, old boy," Ron interrupted.

"Yes," said Maggie. "And, Ron, I was thinking maybe you should stay home from work today, and we can spend some time getting to know Charlie a little better."

"Oh yes," Ron said. "Good idea. Let me call, um, let me call Hoover."

"Good," Maggie said.

"And what business are you in, Ron? May I call you Ron?"

Charlie ventured.

"That's what you always called me before. I mean, that's what the old Charles called me."

"OK. What business are you in, Ron?"

Ron puffed up. "I'm in—"

"Venture capital," Maggie interrupted. "Ron manages our investments."

"Um," said Ron. "Right."

"And he teaches business at Amherst College—just down the road," Maggie continued.

Ron gave Maggie a quizzical look, and Maggie nodded emphatically.

"Right. Yes. What Maggie means to say is I teach part-time at the university," Ron said.

"Managing this estate is a full-time job," Maggie chimed in. Ron puffed out his chest again.

Charlie looked around the room and took in the decor. An untitled watercolor dated 1954. A series of six Japanese wood-block prints. A leaded glass and bronze chandelier.

"Yes, I can only imagine," Charlie said. "And what do you do, Mrs. Vanderough?"

"Please, call me Maggie. Or Mags. You used to call me Mags."

"This Charles does not want to call you Mags!" Ron interjected.

"Maybe he does!"

"As you are the lady of the house," Charlie said calmly,

"and I am your guest, I think it is only appropriate that I call you Mrs. Vanderough."

Maggie blushed. "I manage the household," she said.

"Do you have a large staff?" Charlie asked. *Butlers, maids, footmen, oh my!*

"Actually we have just Sonia and Abel," Maggie said glumly.

"Uh-hum!" Ron cleared his throat. "We don't believe in that old conservative class structure, that upstairs-downstairs nonsense."

"That's right," said Maggie, popping up. "We're not the Kardashians, getting waited on hand and foot twenty-four hours a day. We do things our own way here!"

"Oh," Charlie said.

Maggie rushed to refill Charlie's brandy, and Ron asked, "What have you been up to all these years, Charlie?"

Now it was time to work his magic.

"Well," Charlie began, "I just graduated from the Price-Harold School for Boys."

"Very good school, I hear," said Maggie.

"Right. Yes," said Ron.

"And although Mr. Vanderough—your brother," Charlie said, nodding to Ron, "requested that my existence be kept a secret until my eighteenth birthday, it was his *express wish* that I should reunite with this family upon completion of my studies. He felt it wise that I get acquainted with the family business—that is to say, help manage the family assets."

Ron frowned. Maggie stared blankly.

"Charlie," Ron finally ventured. "How much do you re-member?"

"Remember?" Charlie asked.

"Yes. Do you remember things from your first life?"

Charlie sat dumbfounded. What an absurd question! He found the idea laughable. Were they kidding? Didn't they un-derstand what a clone was? He had no memories of Charles Abernathy Vanderough's former life.

But *they* didn't know that.

"Certain things," Charlie lied. "Like when I saw you, I knew right away that you were my brother. And I remember this house. Ah, this house. I loved this house."

"And me?" cried Maggie. "Do you remember me?"

Hah! He had them fooled. Now it wouldn't be long before Charles Abernathy Vanderough's fortune and estate were un-der his control. It was a wonder at all that Charles Abernathy had left anything in the care of his lunkhead brother and dippy sister-in-law.

"I'm sorry, Mrs. Vanderough," Charlie B said, shaking his head. "You're still blurry to me."

"She's blurry to a lot of people," Ron said. "Don't you worry, my boy. We'll fill you in."

CHAPTER 9

MAGGIE LED CHARLIE up two flights of stairs and down a long hall on the third floor. The manor was in decent shape. Charlie noticed some signs of wear and tear along the way: nicks in the wainscoting, cracks in the ceiling, and stains on the wallpaper. Nothing that a little handiwork couldn't fix. He certainly wouldn't want to stay in this house forever. He'd prefer a penthouse in New York City. Or a mansion in Beverly Hills. Charlie wondered how much a house like this would go for and how soon he could convince Ron and Maggie to put it on the market.

The sound of the radio grew louder as they advanced down the long corridor.

"Ronald's mother still lives with us," Maggie explained. "I guess that makes her your mother too. Do you remember her?"

"Oh yes." Charlie pretended. "Mother."

"Yes. Well, I'm afraid she's not well. She has dementia."

"Oh no," Charlie said. "Poor Mother."

They came to an open door. A small, frail woman sat in a rocking chair with her back to the door and her hand on the knob of an old Sony CFS-67 boom box. Her fingers fumbled with the tuner—a little to the left, a little to the right, back and forth—so that the voice of the radio host went from crackly to clear, crackly to clear.

"Mamma Beth," Maggie called over the static. "Mamma Beth, someone is here to see you."

Maggie led Charlie B into the room and sat him on the little bench inside the dormer window facing the old woman. "Beth, this is Charlie. He's going to be staying with us for a while."

The old woman peered at Charlie through her Rodenstock half-rim glasses.

"Oh Mother," Charlie said dramatically. "It's so good to see you. I've missed you so!"

"Charles," the old woman said. "Home from school already?"

"She remembers you!" Maggie said. "She never remembers me."

"There's apple strudel in the oven if you're hungry," Mamma Beth said, patting her old thighs with the backs of her pruney hands.

"Did you use to cook apple strudel, Mamma Beth?" Maggie interjected. "I bet it was delicious."

"Go fuck yourself!" Mamma Beth barked, folding her arms across her chest.

Maggie just nodded and continued to smile. She leaned over to Charlie and whispered, "She's not very nice."

The old woman turned up the volume on the boom box as high as it would go. Maggie grabbed Charlie's shoulder and said, "That means she wants to be alone."

They retreated into the hallway. Maggie closed the door behind them, shutting out the blaring radio program.

"If we had known you were coming, I'd have asked Sonia to fix up one of the second-floor bedrooms. But I'm afraid this is the only room that's decently furnished."

She led Charlie into a bedroom at the far end of the hall.

"We had a live-in nurse here for a while to take care of Mamma Beth. But we couldn't—" Maggie paused. "What I mean to say is the nurse left. Quite recently."

Maggie looked around anxiously as she spoke, as if she half expected the AWOL nurse to come jumping out from behind a dresser.

"This was her room," Maggie said.

The room was quaint. There was a four-poster canopy bed with gray silk sheets and green velvet curtains embroidered with golden *ombelle* blossoms, a finely carved walnut and marquetry encoignure and matching armoire, a silk floral three-panel folding screen fitted with beveled mirrors, and a carved fruitwood desk "from Berlin," Maggie explained. A blue rotary phone sat on a carved beechwood side table. The bedroom window faced the cedar grove at the back of the house. From there, Charlie could just make out the carriage house to the right of the paved road, and beyond, in the middle of the sweeping lawn, a large willow tree.

"This will suit me fine," Charlie said, trying to sound un-impressed. It was a step up from his tiny dormitory room at Price-Harold. But it wasn't *his*. The room. The furniture. None of it belonged to *him*. At least not yet. Charlie didn't want to give the impression of being *too* comfortable. He still had to find a way to convince Ron and Maggie to hand over what was rightfully his. He may have been just a clone, but if Ron and Maggie really believed he possessed the original Charles's memories too, then what was to stop him from tak-ing hold of the entire estate?

"It isn't quite the same as my old bedroom," Charlie said, thinking on his feet. "I always loved that old bedroom."

"Me too," said Maggie. "I mean—hmm."

"You're in there now, then?"

"Well, yes. Ron and I."

"Hmm." Charlie mused.

"Yes. Well."

Just then, there came the sound of a door opening and clos-ing downstairs, and Ethan called up the landing. "Mom! I need a snack before soccer practice."

Charlie put his leather duffel bag on the floor at the foot of the bed.

"I think I'll take a nap, if you don't mind," he said. "And

I'll join you all for dinner, at say, seven?"

"Oh," said Maggie. "Dinner. Yes. Ethan should be home from practice by then. Yes. Dinner at seven. With the whole family." And she went off mumbling to herself.

Charlie closed the door and turned the key in the lock. It was the first time he'd been alone since he'd knocked on the Vanderough's door at eight o'clock that morning. Ethan had caught the school bus at half past eight. Ron had gotten a call from somebody named Alfredo and had rushed off to manage some affair, no doubt some investment that was rightfully Charlie's. Charlie had been fed a lunch of peanut butter and jelly, and he'd made a show out of what a novelty peanut butter and jelly was for him, even though he'd eaten peanut butter and jelly nearly every week since he was five. Then Maggie had shown Charlie around the house, talking at length about each and every little modernization she and Ron had made, her pitch high and manic, as if confessing to some unspeakable crime. Finally, Charlie had yawned enough times to make it clear that he'd had enough catching up for one morning, and that's when Maggie had finally offered to let him stay at Helmsley House, at least until he found a place of his own in town.

And that was that. Charlie had insinuated himself before anyone could think to look into things properly. How could they know that Charles Abernathy Vanderough had intended to leave Charlie B out of the family fortune?

"How's this for a roof over my head?" Charlie B said to

the ghost of Charles A. Charlie B needn't spend any of his measly pittance on rent and schooling. Instead, he could use the $45,000 to keep up appearances—make everyone believe that he was the most distinguished and well-bred eighteen-year-old in New England.

Charlie fell asleep in the king-size canopy bed, with all the curtains drawn about him to shut out the afternoon sun. He slept for a few hours in the cool, quiet space. Mamma Beth's radio was just a distant murmur beyond the shelter of the silk sheets and velvet curtains. When finally he woke and drew back the curtains, the sun still hovered brightly above the cedar trees. It was only six o'clock in the evening. In this part of the country in the summertime, the sun would not set until 9:00 p.m.

The rotary phone on the side table rang suddenly, shrill and unwelcome. Charlie shivered. He heard Maggie pick up downstairs, her voice coming through the wooden floors as a low, indecipherable rumble. Charlie looked at the phone. If he just picked up the receiver, making sure to cover the transmitter with his hand, he'd be able to listen in without Maggie ever knowing.

He inched over to the phone. Maggie rumbled on down below.

In one swift motion, Charlie removed the handset and covered the transmitter with his palm. Maggie's voice came through clear as a bell.

"I think I can do twelve o'clock on Friday."

"The news isn't good, Maggie," came a man's voice. "This is certainly a setback in your treatment."

Maggie sighed into the transmitter. "Dr. Spritzer, I'm so scared."

"Let's talk about it Friday. Until then, try to take care of yourself."

"Yes, Dr. Spritzer. Thank you."

When they had both hung up, Charlie removed his palm from the transmitter and replaced the handset. Who was Dr. Spritzer, and what was wrong with Maggie? Was she dying? How much time did she have left? Six months? A year? And then what?

A funeral? A reading of the will?

Charlie puzzled over these things for some time before he heard a car coming up the drive. He looked out his window and caught a glimpse of Ron in a yellow Porsche Cayman coupe that looked like it had just come off the lot. The license plate read "Amherst Porsche on Arlington." It had not been fitted with personalized plates yet.

Ron pulled into the carriage house, which had been converted into a six-car garage. When he emerged a few minutes later, he was carrying a small bundle wrapped loosely in a white towel. He held the bundle close to his chest, as if afraid it would suddenly take flight. He entered the house through the back door and disappeared.

Careful not to make any noise, Charlie crept down the long corridor, past Mamma Beth's room, where the radio was now thumping out a hip-hop beat. He could hear Mamma Beth's raspy voice singing along like she had heard the song a hundred times before. Charlie descended two flights of stairs and then made his way noiselessly toward the kitchen, where he could hear Maggie banging around with pots and pans.

And then he caught sight of Ron in the large study—Maggie had called it the den—standing with his back to Charlie, facing a portrait of Winston Churchill. Ron quietly removed the portrait from the wall, revealing a small, steel safe. He turned the knob—right, left, right—and the metal hatch flung open. Ron placed the little bundle in the safe. Then he closed the vault door and rehung the portrait.

Charlie crept back to the stairwell and then made as though he were trundling down the last flight of stairs for the first time.

"Ahoy," Ron said as Charlie came upon him in the den. Ron had moved to the minibar and was pouring himself a drink.

"I bet you could use a whiskey," Ron said, filling another glass.

"Yes, thanks."

"You're a bit young to be drinking," Ron observed. "But I figure you Price-Harold boys know a thing or two about whiskey by the time you graduate."

His tone had become familiar, fatherly.

"Yes, sir," Charlie replied.

"This is a new installment, this home bar. All the latest

amenities in wine and spirits technology."

"Hmm," Charlie murmured, trying to look unimpressed.

"We recently put in a lot of modern appliances. You know, to update the place."

It was a long shot, but Charlie went for it. "You know I never liked the idea of modernizing this house."

Ron stepped back, aghast.

"Charles?" he said. "Is that really you?"

"Of course, Ron," Charlie ventured. "Who else would I be?"

"Charles, do you...I mean, do you remember...everything?"

Charlie felt unsure of himself, uncertain how to proceed. So he backpedaled.

"No, Ron. My memory is still a bit off. Being in this house helps. Seeing Mother. That helped."

"Poor old girl," Ron said, throwing back another whiskey. "Maggie telephoned to tell me how well you and Mother got on today."

"Yes, at least Mother still remembers me."

"And you remember her," Ron said, his ruddy cheeks trembling. "It's a miracle. You really are a miracle."

Then he stopped, put his head on the bar, and whimpered.

"What is it, Ron?"

Ron looked up with salty tears in his eyes.

"Do you remember Maggie yet?"

Charlie worried that Ron would start quizzing him, so he

said, "Not yet."

"Good. It's just as well."

Then Maggie called out from the kitchen.

"Ronald! Ethan! Come quick—and bring the fire extin-guisher."

CHAPTER 10

THEY WERE ALL SEATED around a table at Ming Chen's Chinese Restaurant in downtown Amherst. Maggie had been preparing chicken marsala when the oil in the frying pan had caught fire and set the whole stovetop ablaze. Ethan had come to the rescue with the fire extinguisher. Incidentally, he was taking courses to be an EMT. The fire was extinguished, but dinner was ruined. So they had all piled into Maggie's Porsche Cayenne SUV—Ethan, Charlie, and Mamma Beth in the back and Maggie and Ron in front—and set out for Ming Chen's.

"Don't forget the moo shu pork," Mamma Beth said.

"You love your moo shu pork, don't you, Mamma Beth?" Maggie said.

Mamma Beth rolled her eyes.

"Ethan, no phones at the table!" Ron snatched the iPhone out of Ethan's hands and stuffed it in his pocket.

"So—a large order of moo shu pork, a large order of orange chicken, two orders of shrimp chow mein, a small order of Kung Pao veggies, and rice to go around," Maggie summarized.

The waiter took down the order, and the food arrived within fifteen minutes.

Ethan shoveled chow mein into his mouth and said between bites, "So you're living with us now?"

"No, no. I'm just—" Charlie said.

"Charlie is family," Ron interjected. "He can stay with us as long as he wants. It was your uncle's wish that Charlie here get to know us and become part of the family."

"I didn't even know I had an uncle until this morning," Ethan murmured.

"Well, you know now," Ron said gruffly. "He died before you were born."

"How did he die?" Ethan asked.

Ron and Maggie looked at each other and then looked at Charlie.

"I don't remember that either," Charlie said. He was as eager as Ethan to know the mysterious circumstances surrounding Charles Abernathy Vanderough's death.

"You don't remember anything about it?" Maggie asked.

"No," Charlie said. "But I was young when it happened, wasn't I?"

"Oh Charlie, it was horrible. Terrible." Maggie was on the verge of tears.

"Yes, a tragedy. But I'm sure Charlie doesn't feel like going through it tonight," Ron said.

"Sure he does," Ethan cried.

"I do," Charlie said. "I'd like to know."

Maggie was dabbing the corners of her eyes with the edge of the white linen tablecloth.

"You really don't remember?" She shook her head. "You—"

"Ran your car off the road and slammed into a tree," Ron blurted. "There! I've said it. Now let's eat."

There was a stunned silence at the table. Nobody moved. Maggie stifled a sob. Ethan grimaced.

Then Mamma Beth said, "I thought he shot himself in the head."

"No, Mamma," Ron said, "That was Daddy."

"Oh yes," Mamma Beth said. "Your father always was a good shot."

"Terrible," cried Maggie. "Terrible. Terrible."

Ron was shoveling food onto his plate. "Pass the orange chicken."

Charlie reached across the table and passed the orange chicken.

* * *

That night, Charlie couldn't get the image of a car slamming into a tree out of his head. Only it wasn't Maggie's Porsche SUV or Ron's Cayman coupe. It wasn't any car Charlie recognized. It might have been an old souped-up Toyota Supra or a C4 Corvette—like the one Headmistress Fruth drove. But he wasn't sure. And for some reason, Maggie was beside him in the car, fussing with the radio. They were driving along a dark road. One of his headlamps was out. And then a young man in a gray cardigan appeared in the middle of the road. Charlie swerved to avoid him, and the car slammed headfirst into a maple tree.

Charlie tossed and turned all night, replaying the terrifying scene in his head. The man in the gray cardigan looked familiar. Charlie felt as though he had known him. He searched his memory, sifting through all of the instructors he had had at Price-Harold going back to preschool. Surely he knew this man from somewhere. And the song on the radio, just as he slammed into the tree. What was it? He hummed: "Hmm hm hm hmm hmmmm. Hmm hm hm hmm hmmmm. Hmm hm hm hmm hmmmm—baby…"

It was some old song Charlie had heard before. But he couldn't place it. The chorus kept playing over and over in his head. Maggie fussing with the radio. A young man in a gray cardigan. The big, leafy maple tree.

He rolled over and checked the clock on the nightstand. It was four o'clock in the morning. He hadn't slept a wink. He lay there thinking about what a mess he'd gotten himself into. Two days ago he'd been sitting for his exams at Price-Harold, eager and excited to graduate. And then everything had turned so quickly. He'd read Charles Abernathy's letter. He'd found out that he wasn't the heir to a fortune, but that his inheritance had gone to these two numbskulls who now inhabited Helmsley Park—the estate that should have been his birthright, his home. And now he was playing nice with them, pretending to be someone he wasn't to get a piece of the pie.

"Baby hm hmm hm hmm…" Maggie fussing with the radio. A young man in a gray cardigan. The big, leafy maple tree.

At some point in the early morning, when the sun was already creeping through the mahogany shutters, Charlie finally drifted into unconsciousness.

CHAPTER 11

"**G**OOD MORNING," said Ted Gumbel. "And…"

"Wake up, Boston!" Ted, Caroline, and Raquel cried in unison.

"What a week," said Ted. "Donald Trump announced his presidential bid on Tuesday."

"'See You Again' by Wiz Khalifa topped the pop charts," said Raquel Vasquez.

"Pope Francis caused controversy again," continued Caroline, "by issuing a plea for global action on climate change in an unprecedented encyclical report."

"Nine people are dead from a mass shooting at a predominantly Black church in South Carolina," said Ted. "The suspect, twenty-one-year-old Dylann Storm Roof, is still at large, officials say."

"*Jurassic World* topped the box office last weekend with record-high opening sales."

"The Supreme Court is expected to announce its ruling today on the controversial decision in Texas to reject license plates that feature the Confederate flag."

"Pixar's new film, *Inside Out*, starring Amy Poehler and Mindy Kaling, hits theaters this weekend."

"And what to wear: tips on this summer's hottest styles from fashion correspondent Ashley Mahler."

Ted straightened the papers on his desk. "Let's talk about Donald Trump for a minute. Already, out the gate, he's causing quite a stir in the GOP."

"Yeah," said Caroline. "He's got a lot of people upset."

"He kicked off his presidential campaign this week with a controversial statement about Mexican immigrants. Here's the clip."

A shot of Donald Trump at a podium with a row of American flags in the background flashed on the screen.

"When Mexico sends its people, they're not sending their best. They're not sending you...they're not sending you," Donald Trump said, looking skyward and pointing. "They're sending people that have lots of problems, and they're bringing those problems with us. They're bringing drugs. They're bringing crime. They're rapists. And some, I assume, are good people."

"They're rapists?" asked Ted. "Now that's a sound bite to kick off a campaign."

"Listen," said Raquel. "I understand what he's saying."

"He's—" ventured Caroline.

"No, I get it," Raquel went on. "I get it."

"But isn't he going to alienate voters with a statement like that?" asked Ted.

"I'd still vote for him," said Raquel. "Listen, my parents immigrated here from Mexico. And they went through the proper channels—"

"That's right," interjected Caroline.

"There are ways to become a citizen of the United States," Raquel went on. "Like my parents."

"And if you're not a citizen, then you aren't voting anyway, right?" said Ted.

"Right!" said Caroline.

"So who's he alienating?" Raquel asked, looking squarely into the camera. "Not me."

"We have another clip," said Ted.

Another shot of Trump at the podium filled the screen.

"I would build a great wall, and nobody builds walls better than me—believe me," said Trump. "And I'll build them very inexpensively. I will build a great, great wall on our southern border. And I will have Mexico pay for that wall."

"Do we really need a wall?" asked Ted.

"That's not the point," said Caroline. "It's the idea. Something has to be done."

"I completely agree," said Raquel.

"OK, so what about last night," said Ted, changing the subject. "A man walks into a predominantly Black church where a Bible study is taking place. He sits for a while. And then opens fire on the group and kills nine people."

"Awful, just terrible."

"Apparently, there is evidence to suggest this young man was a white supremacist sympathizer."

"How did someone like that get ahold of a gun?"

"I say we get a list of all the white supremacists and illegal immigrants and Muslims and ban them from purchasing firearms."

"You mean Muslim extremists," Ted corrected.

"Yes, people who sympathize with the Islamic State."

"It's not about gun control," interjected Raquel. "It's about who we're letting into this country."

"Apparently, the suspect of last night's shooting is still at large, and officials are asking anybody who sees this man, Dylann Roof, to call the police immediately."

A picture of a young white man with a bowl cut flashed on the screen.

"So," Ted began again, "who saw *Jurassic World* this weekend?"

CHAPTER 12

CHARLIE WOKE UP to the sound of Maggie's voice on the drive below. He shuffled over to the window and peered down. Maggie stood outside on the lawn in her bathrobe. Ron was on the asphalt drive in a suit holding a briefcase. Maggie was pleading with him.

"Please!" she said. "I can't do it any longer. Please just let me!"

"Hush," Ron said. "Not until we know more."

"But it's eating away at me!"

"I don't like it any more than you do. But it's for everybody's good."

"But—"

"Listen to me, Maggie," Ron hissed. "Your instincts were right from the beginning. You started this, and now you've got to finish it. I've talked to Ethan. I've talked to Sonia. It's all settled."

Maggie was still standing on the lawn, shoulders slumped, arms at her sides. "And what did you tell them?"

"Never mind that," Ron said. "They won't say a thing."

There was a sudden knock on the bedroom door. Charlie leaped back into bed and pulled the covers up to his chin.

"Yes?" he said. "Come in."

The door opened, and a tall, thin Latina woman came in carrying a pile of freshly folded white towels.

"Sorry to disturb you," she said. "Mrs. Vanderough asked me to bring you some fresh towels."

Her face was long and angular. She had broad shoulders and a cleft chin. But she was young—couldn't be more than twenty-five. She kept her eyes down and moved across the room to the wooden desk.

"I'll leave these here for you," she said.

"Thank you."

As she was leaving the room, she looked up for just a moment and met Charlie's eyes. She stared. Then she turned on her heel and hurried out of the room, closing the door behind her.

By the time Charlie was back at the window, Ron was gone, and Maggie was alone on the lawn clutching her sides and sobbing.

Charlie looked at the clock. It was 10:00 a.m. Ethan would be at school already. Ron was off to manage the family portfolio. Charlie could hear the radio down the hall playing what he would eventually learn was Mamma Beth's favorite morning show: *Rightwing with Bill Richardson*. He could hear a vacuum running somewhere two floors below—he assumed that was Sonia.

Charlie washed up in the private bath and headed downstairs. His head was killing him, and he needed coffee desperately. When he arrived in the kitchen, there was already a handyman working on the charred countertops around the blackened stove. Maggie came through the back door and found Charlie sitting at the little dinette in the corner of the kitchen.

"I'll get you some coffee," she said, wiping the tears away.

There was a small Panasonic television above the refrigerator. Maggie flicked it on absentmindedly. A show called *Wake Up, Boston!* was on HBC. The sounds of the host's and hostesses' voices pierced through Charlie's skull like electric drills.

"How do you take your coffee, Charlie?" Maggie asked, revving up the shiny new Keurig 2.0. "Don't need the stove to make coffee anymore," she said. "You always said the day we got a coffeemaker was the day we sold this house."

"We?"

"I mean *you*. I was always trying to convince *you* to modernize. You hated the idea. You said that modern appliances don't suit an old house like this one."

"And have you ever considered selling the house?" Charlie probed. "Now that you've got a coffeemaker."

"Oh never. I could never sell this house. Ron wants me to. But it's *my* house after all."

"Your house?"

"Mm, yes." Maggie hesitated. "Well, it's in my name. That's all. It's as much Ron's as it is mine, I guess."

She handed Charlie a cup of coffee and asked, "Did you hear about the church shooting last night? It's all over the news." And with that, she turned the volume up on the television set, indicating that the conversation was over and they'd be watching Ted, Caroline, and Raquel prattle on about some shooting down in the backwoods of South Carolina. Charlie couldn't be bothered. He had to think of a way to get Maggie to tell him more about the house. *Charles Abernathy Vanderough had left the house in Maggie's name?* What else had he left her? How much of the Vanderough fortune was in her name? Why her and not Ron?

Charlie was deep in contemplation when the handyman said, "All right, Mrs. V. Everything is in working order. Just don't leave the burners unattended again. My ex-wife burned down our whole duplex that way."

"Thank you, Steven," Maggie said, switching off the television set. "How much do I owe you?"

"This one's on the house. After the deal Ron got me on—"

"Steven, you know how much I hate to talk about business," Maggie said abruptly.

"Sorry, Mrs. V. I won't mention it again. Anyway, I gotta

be going. Mrs. Delaney up the road has a busted pipe."

Then Steven the handyman turned to Charlie and extended his hand.

"I'm sorry. We haven't met yet. I'm Steven Oden. Town handyman. You are?"

"Um—"

"His name is Chris," Maggie blurted. "He's an exchange student from California."

"Nice to meet you, Chris," said Steven. "It's funny, but I feel like we've met before."

"Couldn't have," Maggie said. "This is Chris's first time on the East Coast."

"Welcome. School's almost out for the summer, isn't it?"

"Gets out tomorrow," Maggie said.

"Hey," Steven said. "Why aren't you at school now?"

"Head cold," Charlie said, taking Maggie's lead. And then he coughed loudly.

"Well, you better take it easy."

"And you'd better get along to see about Mrs. Delaney's pipes," Maggie said, ushering Steven the handyman out the back door.

* * *

"Whew," she said when she came back in. "That was close. He almost recognized you. Do you remember Steven?"

"Steven Oden," Charlie said, giving it a shot. "From high

school?"

"Right! Oh, your memory is coming back." Then she hesitated. "Do you remember *me* from high school?"

"No," Charlie said, still afraid she'd catch him in the lie. "You and I went to school together?"

Maggie's eyes were still red from when she had been crying. They welled up again. She brushed aside the tears and said, "Allergies."

Then she continued, staring into her cup of coffee. "Everybody in this town went to high school together. And then to college together. If they even went to college."

"Did you?" Charlie asked. "Go to college, I mean?"

"I studied a year at Amherst," she said. "And you went off to Yale. Everybody was so proud of you."

Just then, Charlie remembered what Charles Abernathy had said in his letter—how he regretted never getting a proper education.

"But I didn't finish," he said to Maggie.

"That's right!" Maggie said. "It's funny what you can remember."

"Why didn't I finish?" Charlie asked.

Maggie's eyes were swollen. She looked away. "It's a long story. I'd rather not discuss it." And then Maggie switched on the television set again. A woman named Ashley Mahler appeared on the screen beside a makeshift runway. Men and women who had been plucked out of the live audience strutted up and down the aisle.

"The denim jacket is back in style this year. And hats, hats, hats. The bolder, the better."

Maggie seemed to disappear into the program, her eyes glued to the screen. Charlie sipped his coffee and stared out the bay window. There was an old Dodge Ram parked in the drive. The bed of the pickup truck was loaded with gardening supplies piled six feet high: hedge clippers, hose extensions, leaf blowers, push brooms, rakes, shovels, ladders, chain saws, buzz saws, handsaws, oh my! The driver of the pickup was nowhere to be seen.

When the fashion segment had ended and the conversation on *Wake Up, Boston!* had turned to the Pope's call for action on climate change, Maggie broke from her trance and turned to face Charlie.

"I have an idea," she said, smiling. "Why don't we go into Boston this weekend and do a little shopping?"

"Um," Charlie said.

"It'll be fun," Maggie pressed. "Ron has to work all weekend. Ethan can watch Mamma Beth. It'll be just you and me."

"OK."

"We'll take my car. It's only a two-hour drive to Boston. If we leave early Saturday morning, then we can be back in time for dinner."

At Price-Harold, Charlie had taken class trips into New York City every year to see the ballet and visit museums. But Boston was totally unknown to him.

"I've never been to Boston," he said.

"Great! A summer shopping spree! My treat."

* * *

After a breakfast of oatmeal and eggs, Maggie excused herself to her bedroom, claiming to have a headache. Charlie was left alone in the kitchen. He had yet to see the full extent of the grounds at Helmsley Park, so he decided to take a mid-morning stroll. It was a perfect day. The temperature on the little digital thermometer on the kitchen stoop read seventy-three degrees Fahrenheit. The humidity was low, and a cool breeze swept away whatever discomfort the humidity might have wrought.

Paper-thin cirrus clouds striated the cool blue sky. Charlie made his way out onto the lawn, past the carriage house and the willow tree, and toward a low, squat glass building he hadn't noticed before.

As Charlie came upon the tidy barrack, he saw at once that it was a greenhouse for fruit trees, vegetables, and flowers. Several avocado trees stood in a row just inside the glass doors. One door was ajar, so he stepped inside and looked around.

That was when Charlie first saw the woman: wide hips, broad shoulders, one long dark braid down her back, round brown eyes, soft red lips.

Charlie ducked behind an avocado tree. The woman moved through the rows of the greenhouse, her fingers caressing the budding plants. At the end of a long aisle, there was an open door leading into a cool, dark shed. When the woman was framed in the doorway of the shed, the sunlight reflecting off her white dress, she began to disrobe. She undressed with her back to Charlie, her dress slipping off her shoulders. Charlie stood transfixed.

Once the dress had dropped to the floor, she unhooked her bra and took off her panties so that her full form was exposed. Still she had not noticed Charlie.

The woman began to unbraid her hair, slowly, methodically. The muscles in her thighs and buttocks tensed and relaxed as each twist of the braid came undone. As she undid the final twist in the braid, she shook her head, and the hair splayed out along her broad back.

Only then did she turn and see Charlie. But instead of screaming—instead of running for the hills—she smiled. Then she scooped up her apparel and stepped into the shadow of the cool, dark shed.

Charlie guessed then that the woman must have known all along that he was there watching. And it seemed to Charlie that she wanted him to follow her. Charlie slid out from behind the avocado tree. He made his way down a row of asphodels and stepped into the shed.

It was empty. Not a soul to be found. The space was tiny, no bigger than a water closet. There were no other doors. No windows.

Where had she gone?

Charlie stepped out of the shed and searched behind rows of tulips and cabbages and strawberries. When he finally left the building, he walked a full circle around the barrack. Still no sign of the mysterious woman.

He left the greenhouse feeling flummoxed. The woman had played some kind of trick on him. A disappearing act like the great Houdini. He'd been had. Duped. Hoodwinked. Conned. Charlie felt embarrassed and angry. Had someone set him up? Were they watching him now through a spyglass? He examined the dozens of windows of Helmsley House, looking for some phantom to reveal itself.

Where was she?

Charlie vowed to go back to the greenhouse at a less conspicuous hour, to check for trapdoors and secret passageways. An old house like this was bound to have hidden rooms.

As Charlie tromped back to the house, he passed the gardener mowing the lawn. The gardener was a short, squat Latino man in baggy blue jeans and a sweat-stained T-shirt. His mustache was streaked with gray.

The old gardener looked up at Charlie as he passed, and their eyes met. The gardener stopped dead in his tracks. The mower idled. He stood still as stone, watching Charlie with his deep-set eyes.

"Hello," Charlie said.

The man said nothing.

Charlie turned and continued on. When he reached the back door of the house, he turned to look at the gardener once more. The old man was still standing in the middle of the green lawn, the mower idling, his hands at his sides, staring at Charlie.

Charlie was unnerved. He stepped into the quiet comfort of Helmsley House, knowing the gardener could not follow him there.

Charlie made his way up the first flight of stairs, where he met the lanky, horse-faced Sonia on the first-floor landing. Her sudden appearance startled him, and he cried out. Sonia cocked her head like a hen, looked at Charlie with her big round eyes, and then, without saying a word, continued down the stairs, carrying a basketful of dirty laundry.

When Charlie reached the second-floor landing, he heard Maggie calling out to him.

"Charlie. Is that you?"

"Yes," Charlie said.

"Can you come here for a second?"

Charlie made his way down the hall to the primary bedroom on the second floor. Maggie was lying in an adjustable king-size bed. Her knees were bent at 110 degrees, and her torso was nearly upright. She had on a pair of reading glasses and was peering over the top of a copy of Arthur Golden's *Memoirs of a Geisha*.

"Somebody telephoned for you," she said, "but I couldn't find you."

"What? Who?"

"He wouldn't say. He just asked if I knew a Charlie B Vanderough. I said I did and that I'd be happy to take a message. But he said not to bother. He'd try back later."

Who was calling Charlie here? Who even knew that Charlie was in Massachusetts? Not that many people even knew he existed, for that matter.

"How did he get the number for Helmsley Park?" Charlie asked.

"We're publicly listed," Maggie said.

"OK," Charlie said. "I'll be in my room if he calls again."

Charlie went up to his room and flopped down on the bed. He stared a long time at the blue rotary phone, willing it to ring. He fantasized that he would get a call from one of Charles Abernathy's old attorneys. An executor of the will. And he would tell Charlie that he had been had. Duped. Hoodwinked. Conned. Somehow, Maggie and Ron had played a sick joke on him, and Charlie was to inherit $100 million in stocks and bonds.

Butlers, maids, footmen, oh my!

Charlie turned over on his side and tucked his feet up under his legs. Soon, he was asleep, and the terrible visions from the previous night came roaring back to him. Driving along a dark country road. Maggie fussing with the radio. A young man in a gray cardigan appearing in the light of a single headlamp. The trunk of a giant maple tree.

Charlie awoke to the shrill ring of the telephone. The sun was still shining through the windows. He leaped out of bed and picked up the receiver.

"Hullo?" he said.

"Hello. This is Dr. Spritzer. Is Mrs. Vanderough available?"

"Oh," Charlie said, disappointed. Then Maggie picked up the other line.

"Hello?" she said into the phone.

"Mrs. Vanderough," said Dr. Spritzer. "Hello."

"Oh, Dr. Spritzer. So nice to hear your voice again."

"I'll hang up now," Charlie said. He covered the transmitter with the palm of his hand and tapped the switch hook. Then he waited breathlessly on the line.

Dr. Spritzer continued. "I just wanted to call to let you know that I did some extensive research after our last conversation, and I think I may be able to help."

"Oh yes, Dr. Spritzer. Whatever you say. You know I'll do whatever it takes."

"Great. We can discuss it at our appointment tomorrow."

"Oh, Dr. Spritzer, you're a lifesaver!" Maggie exclaimed.

And with a few words of farewell, they ended the conversation.

Charlie hung up the receiver and flopped back on the bed. He looked at the clock. It was already 4:00 p.m. He had napped most of the day away. His experience with the woman in the greenhouse still haunted him.

Mamma Beth's radio blared from down the hall. Charlie could just make out the news story. Apparently, the South Carolina church shooter, Dylann Storm Roof, had been caught thanks to a civilian do-gooder who'd spotted the suspect. The reporter was describing the horror that had unfolded in the church the previous evening. Mamma Beth cranked up the volume a few notches.

What was Charlie doing there? He felt like a prisoner. He didn't want to leave his room for fear of running into Maggie again. Mamma Beth's radio never let up. Sonia kept coming and going in the hall, banging linen cupboard doors. And from his window, Charlie could see the stoic gardener out in the yard sweeping the dust and pollen from the drive. For such a big house, there was no place to hide.

But he didn't want to stay in this room forever. He was growing bored. He hadn't been on a computer since he left Price-Harold. He wasn't even sure Ron and Maggie owned a computer. For all their talk of modernization, Helmsley House was strangely isolated with a single landline and no Internet to speak of.

At Price-Harold, the students weren't allowed to keep computing devices in the dormitories, so Charlie didn't own a phone or computer, either. It was part of the deal of being a clone. Instead, they had had round-the-clock access to a state-of-the-art computer lab. Charlie had spent many of his evenings in the library at Price-Harold with other clones browsing the Internet for news of their donors.

Charlie was shaken from his reverie by the sound of a car horn in the drive.

Bleep! Bleeeeeeep!

He looked out the window. Ron was standing in the yard with a brand-new Porsche Boxster convertible.

Bleeeeeeeep!

"What in God's name?" he heard Maggie say from somewhere down below.

"It's here! It's here!" Ethan cried, bursting onto the lawn and running circles around the car.

"Where's Charlie?" Ron asked. He cried out, "Charlie, get down here!"

Charlie hustled down the stairs and out the back door. Sonia was now standing on the lawn with Maggie. The gardener had disappeared somewhere. Ethan was already in the driver's seat of the Boxster with the top down, revving the engine.

"Dear Lord," said Maggie. "What on earth was Ron thinking?" She was standing beside Sonia, arms folded across her chest. Ron was hovering over Ethan, pointing out all of the car's exciting features.

"Ron!" she called across the lawn. "What on earth were you thinking?"

"It's an end-of-term present for Ethan," he called back.

"But he doesn't even have a permit yet."

"We made a deal!" cried Ethan.

"Shut up, Ethan," Ron barked. "Let's talk basics: you've got your gearshift here, and your emergency brake. Charlie, get over here."

Charlie meandered across the lawn and caught sight of the

gardener lingering in the shadow of the willow tree.

"That's just Abel," Ron said. "Abel! What do you think?"

Abel nodded.

"Doesn't speak a lick of English." Ron chuckled. "You ready to go for a ride?"

"Sure," Charlie said. "But there are only two seats."

"Yeah," said Ron. "One for you, and one for Ethan. I don't need to go with you. Ethan knows the drill. Just once around the block, eh?"

"All right," said Ethan, putting the car in drive. "Get in, Charlie."

Charlie hopped in and buckled his seat belt. Maggie waved good-bye. Sonia stood motionless at her side. Ron patted the car on the trunk and said, "Giddyup," and the car took off like a bat out of hell. Ethan spun around in the driveway at full speed and headed up the drive. Up ahead, the gate was propped open with a big granite rock. Ethan sped right through and onto Rolling Hills Way, not stopping to check for oncoming traffic.

"Shit!" said Ethan. "This baby can move!"

Shit, indeed. They sped down the country road for what seemed like ages, Ethan using the opposite lane to pass every car going under eighty miles per hour. Big colonials and Victorians whizzed by, their yards lush with oaks and cedars and maples. Charlie gripped the side of his seat tightly. Ethan flipped on the radio and blasted 105.3 FM, "Amherst's first stop for classic rock."

Then Ethan's phone beeped. He pulled it out of his pocket and started texting.

"Ethan," Charlie said, gritting his teeth as they zoomed past a truck full of squawking chickens. "Ethan, can you...maybe...not text while you drive?"

"Uh-huh," Ethan said, not looking up from his phone for more than a few seconds at a time.

"I think we should head back now," Charlie said.

"Uh-huh."

Ethan rounded a corner at fifty miles an hour. Then Charlie saw it. A giant red maple tree with big leafy branches. It wasn't just any maple tree. This was the same maple tree that he kept seeing in his nightmares. And this was the road. And right there was the spot where the young man in the gray cardigan had been standing. A wave of nausea washed over him.

"Ethan," Charlie cried. "Stop. I'm going to be sick."

"What?" Ethan said, still looking at his phone.

Charlie leaned out the window and puked. The vomit splattered all over the side of the car.

Ethan screeched to a maddening halt. "What the hell, Charlie!"

Charlie leaped out of the car and bent over an irrigation ditch on the side of the road and vomited again. Ethan examined the side of his car. A long streak of muddy bile extended from the passenger door to the taillight.

"Disgusting," Ethan muttered.

"Go home without me," Charlie said. "I'll walk."

"We're like ten miles from home," Ethan said. "You can't walk!"

"You wanna bet," Charlie said. "Tell your parents I got carsick."

"Shit," said Ethan. "I'm sorry—"

"Shut up," Charlie said. "You could have killed us. I need to be alone for a while."

"Jeez," said Ethan. "You sound like my dad. OK. Do you have a phone or something in case you get lost?"

"I'm not going to get lost."

Ethan got into the coupe, made a quick U-turn in the middle of the road, and zoomed off. Charlie waited until the car was out of sight to approach the big maple tree. There was a large scar around its trunk that had healed over with smooth, pale bark. He searched the surrounding area for other signs of a car crash. There was a low wire fence bordering the adjacent field. A section of the fence was missing just beyond the maple tree. Charlie walked over and noted that the wires had been yanked clean off the wooden posts.

Charlie knelt at the edge of the field and vomited again. After about ten minutes, when his stomach had finally settled, he got up and began the long walk back to Helmsley Park. There was a part of him that didn't want to go back. He imagined disappearing without a trace. Let Ron and Maggie and Ethan think he was dead. He could do that: disappear without a trace. The world had no record of him.

All Charlie had to do was knock on one of these colonial

doors, ask to use a phone, and call a cab to get him the hell out of there.

But where would he go? Charlie didn't have a home. He didn't have a job. His pitiful inheritance wasn't enough to last him through the year. At Helmsley House, Charlie had been given free room and board. A place to be. A family. Charlie wasn't ready to divorce himself from the only lifeline he had left. Not yet, anyway.

He trudged along the side of the road, cars zooming past, their drivers eying him with suspicion. Then a black Porsche Cayenne SUV pulled up beside Charlie. It was Maggie.

"I'm so sorry it took me so long. I was dropping Ron off at the dealership so he could pick up his car when Ethan called me. He told me what happened."

"It's all right," Charlie said. "I was just going to walk home."

"It's too far to walk," she said. "Get in." Then she added, "Ethan is heating up a frozen pizza. We'll have dinner when we get back."

"OK."

"I don't know what Ron was thinking," Maggie said, when Charlie was finally in the car and they were on their way back to Helmsley Park. "He knows Ethan is not ready to drive on his own."

"What was the deal he made with Ron?" Charlie asked. "To get the car?"

"Oh, never mind that. It was stupid. Ron and I cave in too

easily to Ethan's demands."

Demands, Charlie thought. *What demands, exactly?*

They drove on in silence for some time. Finally, Maggie spoke.

"Tomorrow I have to go into town to run a few errands."

Charlie remembered Maggie's noontime doctor's appointment. "Is everything OK?" he asked.

"Of course! I have to pick up groceries. And get my hair done." Her voice was high and pitchy. Charlie was quickly learning that Maggie was a terrible liar.

"I need to ask a favor of you," she continued.

"Uh-huh."

"Sonia can't come in tomorrow. Ron will be at work, and Ethan will be at school. So I was wondering if you could watch Mamma Beth while I'm gone."

"Oh," Charlie said. He'd completely forgotten about Mamma Beth.

"You just need to look in on her every once in a while. I'll make sure she eats before I leave. And I should be back before Ethan gets home."

"Sure," Charlie said. Then he remembered the woman in the greenhouse. "Will anybody else be at the house tomorrow? The gardener?"

"No," Maggie said. "He and Sonia always come together. Abel is Sonia's father."

"Oh. Does anyone else ever help around the house?" Charlie asked, trying to sound casual.

"No," Maggie said, thinking. "We haven't been able to keep anyone."

"Hmm."

Then Maggie added, "At least not since Ynez died."

CHAPTER 13

MAGGIE EXPLAINED that Ynez was Sonia's mother. For thirty years, Ynez had worked at Helmsley Park. When Charles Abernathy Vanderough bought the estate in 1981, Ynez and her husband, Abel, showed up in a blue Jeep pickup. Apparently, the young couple had been working at the house for years, but nobody had bothered to tell them that the estate was transferring hands. So they just turned up one day and set to work as usual, not knowing that their original employers had flown the coop.

Charles Abernathy took pity on them and asked them to stay on—as he needed a maid and a gardener anyway. And so Ynez and Abel continued on as they always had, keeping everything in order. They gave birth to Sonia in 1992, and by the time she was ten, little Sonia was already helping her mother clean the house.

Ynez died suddenly of a heart attack in 2005. She had been in the middle of cleaning the toilet in the primary bedroom. Sonia had been downstairs scrubbing the kitchen sink. They found Ynez slumped over the toilet clutching a squeegee, her body already stiff from rigor mortis.

Since then, it had been only Sonia and Abel, Maggie explained. They had hired a live-in nurse for Mamma Beth for a while, a German woman called Frau Merkel. But Frau Merkel had left recently for reasons Maggie didn't want to go into.

And so Charlie had inherited the Frau's room—and apparently her job too.

"Mamma Beth is really easy," Maggie said, assuring him after dinner that night. "I'll only be gone for a few hours tomorrow. You just have to make sure she has her radio and a glass of whiskey, and she won't cause you any bother."

"Show me where the whiskey is," Charlie said.

The following morning, Maggie served up a heaping plate of bacon, eggs, and hash browns with a cup of black coffee. Charlie had slept straight through to nine o'clock; it was the first decent sleep he'd gotten since he'd left Price-Harold. Ethan and Ron were already out of the house when Charlie awoke, so he spent the morning with Maggie sitting at the little dinette watching Ted, Caroline, and Raquel bicker about ObamaCare and bikini waxes on *Wake Up, Boston!* Then, around quarter to eleven, Maggie headed out the back door and left Charlie alone in the house with Mamma Beth.

Charlie got to work immediately. Mamma Beth's radio was up as loud as it would go; a program called *What Would Jesus Do?* had just begun. It would be at least thirty minutes before he would need to check in on her. So he started in Ron's den.

Charlie sifted through the papers on Ron's desk: a catalog for Macy's, an insurance claim for Dr. Spritzer, M.D., totaling $950, a coupon for a free car wash at Amherst Porsche on Arlington, a receipt for a Weber Q1400 1,560-watt electric grill, and a bill from Verizon Wireless for a family text and call plan.

There was a two-drawer file cabinet in the den, but it was locked. And when Charlie checked the drawers in the oak desk, he found only pens, pencils, pictures of Ethan as a little boy, and paper clips. Ron had several family photographs on display next to his diploma from Amherst College, but none of the photographs was of Charles Abernathy Vanderough.

Charlie moved on to the large dining room, then to the kitchen, the laundry room, and the family room, and finally found himself back in the parlor where he had first sat with Ron and Maggie drinking brandy at eight o'clock in the morning. There was no evidence of Charles Abernathy Vanderough's existence anywhere to be found. No portraits. No photo albums. No nothing. There were a few photos on the walls featuring Mamma Beth, never as a young woman, but as she was now: demented and bent with age.

Charlie was thumbing through coffee table books in the

parlor when he noticed something odd. The big watercolor that had been on the wall on the day of his arrival was gone. There was a faint outline on the wall where the painting had been. Then he noticed other things were missing too: the carved mahogany settee, the upholstered club chair, and the Victorian needlepoint rug.

The parlor had been warm and cramped the day he arrived, but now it felt empty and hollow.

Just as he was about to head upstairs to investigate the bedrooms, Charlie noticed a closed door in the parlor that Maggie had left off the tour. He tried the handle. It was unlocked. On the other side was a high-ceilinged library with floor-to-ceiling bookcases. There was a comfy round library settee in the middle of the room and a long table with vintage brass desk lamps arrayed neatly along its length. The windows in this room were stained glass, blue and red and yellow. A chandelier hung from the vaulted ceiling.

And there on the wall above a darkened fireplace, centered between two stained-glass windows, was a painted portrait of a young man in a gray cardigan. He was standing squarely against a canvas of gray and black. Charlie gasped and felt the nausea come over him again. He steadied himself in the door frame. Only once he was sure that the worst of the nausea had passed did he creep over to the portrait and read the attribution: Franz H. Vanderough.

"It's beautiful, isn't it," said a voice behind him.

Charlie jumped.

Mamma Beth was standing in the doorway.

"That's your father when he was about your age," she said. "His mother, your grandmother, knew Andrew Wyeth's wife, Betsy. Andrew Wyeth agreed to paint your father for a modest fee. Your father and I were married shortly after that portrait was done."

Mamma Beth stood staring at the portrait. Her mouth twitched involuntarily, but her gaze was steady and fixed.

"He should be home from Kenya soon," she said.

"Yes," Charlie said, wanting her to go on, to tell him everything she knew.

"I'm so proud of you, Charles," she said. "Your father always knew you'd turn out to be a Yale man."

"Thank you, Mamma," Charlie said, playing along.

"Where's Ynez?" Mamma Beth asked suddenly, her gaze breaking from the portrait.

"What?"

"Ynez! Ynez!" Mamma Beth looked frantic. She clawed at the door frame, clinging to it as if it were a life preserver.

"She'll be right in," Charlie lied. "Ynez is coming."

"When?" Mamma Beth demanded. "I need her now!"

"She'll be here any minute," Charlie said, hoping to calm the old matron. "We can wait for her upstairs."

"Who?" Mamma Beth said.

He took her by the hand and guided her to the stairs. Together, they ascended the flights one at a time. Mamma Beth was extraordinarily spry. She kept looking around for Ynez as she climbed. On the first-floor landing, she started calling for Franz, so Charlie said, "Father's still in Kenya. He'll be home tomorrow."

"Oh Charles," she said. "You're home from school."

"Yes, Mamma. Yes."

And it went on like this all the way up to the third floor where they caught the end of *What Would Jesus Do?* playing on the radio.

Once Charlie got Mamma Beth in her chair, she calmed down. She put her hand on the dial of the radio—turning it a little to the right and then a little to the left—until finally she fell asleep.

Charlie spent the next hour exploring the rest of the house. There were six bedrooms on the second floor and another four on the third floor, counting his own and Mamma Beth's. At the opposite end of the hall on the third floor was a single locked door. It was the only door in the house that Charlie couldn't open. *It must lead to the attic,* Charlie thought.

Charlie got down on his hands and knees and peered through the space under the door. There was a cold draft coming from the other side. All he could see was darkness.

Charlie looked around for a set of keys, trying Ron's den again and searching the downstairs closets. There were a few keys lying around—mostly spares for the family's myriad Porsches. There was an old skeleton key in Ron's desk drawer, but it didn't fit the lock of the mysterious third-floor door.

Then Charlie remembered the hidden safe. He returned to Ron's den, put the skeleton key back where he'd found it, and removed the portrait of Winston Churchill from the wall. There was a gray outline where the portrait had hung framing the black combination safe. Charlie tried the little hatch on the safe. It was locked tightly in place. He fiddled with the combination dial for a bit, listening carefully for a click or a whir to tell him whether he was turning it in the right direction, but the hatch didn't budge.

Finally, he gave up and returned Churchill to his place on the wall, made sure everything in Ron's den was exactly as it had been before he'd begun snooping around, and retired to the library to get another look at the portrait of Franz Vanderough.

How had this man ended up in his dreams? he wondered. Charlie had never seen the portrait before today. At least not that he could remember.

No, there was no way he'd seen the portrait of Franz Vanderough before. It must have been a coincidence that the man in his dreams, the man he swerved to avoid before crashing into the maple tree, looked so much like the man in the portrait, the family patriarch. In fact, the man in his dreams was hardly more than a blur. There was no sure way to know that he looked identical to Franz Vanderough.

Nevertheless, the portrait fascinated Charlie. This was the man who had fathered Charles Abernathy Vanderough and whose genetic material made up half of Charlie's DNA.

Franz Vanderough had shot himself in the head. That's what Mamma Beth had said at Ming Chen's Chinese Restaurant that first night. And Charles Abernathy Vanderough, his son, had driven head-on into a tree.

It seemed the men in this family didn't have much luck.

* * *

When Maggie returned from her errands later that day, Charlie noted that her hair was exactly as it had been before she left and that she had no groceries to speak of—clearly she had visited neither the hairdresser nor the market. Charlie said nothing of it, however. He pretended to know nothing about her noon appointment with Dr. Spritzer and her mysterious medical condition.

Maggie seemed cheerful enough, though. She kept talking about their imminent trip to Boston and couldn't wait to show Charlie all her favorite spots.

"Do you remember anything about Boston?" she probed. "Do you remember the old studio apartment on Hanover?"

"I remember baked beans," Charlie said, knowing from regional lore that Boston was famous for its baked beans.

"Oh, you hated baked beans," Maggie said, laughing.

"Ech." Charlie retched.

"Sometimes you sound just like the old Charles," Maggie said, growing pensive. "And sometimes it's like you're a stranger in his body."

The expression *a wolf in lamb's clothing* came to mind, but Charlie dared not say it out loud. Instead he said, "Oh Maggie. You've been so good to me. I wish I could remember *you* better."

Maggie looked away. "It's probably best you don't," she said and switched on the kitchen television set.

CHAPTER 14

"**Y**EAH!" **BRIAN CRIED,** slamming his paddle on the table. "Ten to eight. Game point!"

"Bring it on, Glazier," Mike Chapman said. A blue and yellow ping-pong table bridged the distance between the two men.

"Serving," Brian called. And he whacked the little ping-pong ball over the net where it bounced off the corner of the table and into a nearby trashcan.

"Dammit!" Mike said. "You win again, Glazier. How much time do you spend up here? You're a pro."

"I like to put in a good two hours a day when I can," Brian said proudly.

Mike went to retrieve the ball. As he crossed the hall, he nearly collided with a scruffy young guy in a puffer jacket riding by on a hoverboard.

"Whoa! Sorry, Miles!" Mike said as the hoverboard

whizzed by.

The kid on the hoverboard called back as he glided down the hall, "Watch where you're going, asshole!"

"Who the hell was that?" Brian asked.

"New intern," said Mike. "I get a weird vibe from him."

"He's an entitled punk," Brian concluded. "Kids are shits these days."

The two men headed into a small kitchenette just off the rec room. Mike opened the fridge. Inside, there were rows and rows of bottled, canned, and boxed drinks.

"Can I get a coconut water?" Brian asked, wiping the sweat from his brow.

"Sure thing," Mike said, grabbing two juice boxes.

"So is the sampler out yet?" Brian stabbed his straw into the top of the box.

"Not yet. We're still trying to get Taylor Swift and Adele to sign on. We're getting a lot of resistance from their people."

"You'll let me know when it's out?" Brian asked.

"Don't I always?" Mike sipped through his narrow straw.

"Did you hear they're gonna have Trump's campaign people here to speak on the twenty-fifth?" Brian asked.

"Are you into that guy?" Mike asked skeptically.

"Abso-fucking-lutely," Brian said. "Who else is gonna look out for American jobs?"

"And build a wall along the southern border?"

"You want every rapist in Latin America pounding down our doors?"

"That's fucked up," Mike said.

"I call it like it is. You got a problem with that?"

Mike chuckled. "That's why I love you, Brian."

"I love you too, bro."

"OK, I gotta get back to work. I have a meeting with Brenda downstairs at eleven."

"OK," Brian said. "Meet you at the air hockey table at two?"

CHAPTER 15

THE FOLLOWING MORNING, Charlie awoke to the familiar blare of Mamma Beth's radio. Maggie and he were to set off to Boston by 8:00 a.m. Charlie showered and dressed and hurried downstairs where he joined Ron and Ethan in the kitchen.

"So you're off to ol' Beantown," Ron said. "Need some new clothes for the summer? Maybe some new shoes?"

"Yes."

"I'm sorry I won't be joining you," Ron continued. "I could use the drive. I love a nice long drive. Maybe you can take Ethan's convertible, since it'll just be the two of you."

"Dad!" Ethan cried, looking up from his phone for the first time since Charlie had sat down next to him at the table. "That's not fair. It's my car. What if Mom bangs it up?"

"Your mother is not going to *bang it up*," Ron barked. "You were more likely to do that on your joyride the other night. It's lucky you didn't slam into a tree."

Charlie cringed.

Ethan huffed.

Maggie arrived in the kitchen a few minutes later, her thinning auburn hair in ringlets around her shoulders, a pearl necklace around her thick neck, and dressed in a freshly pressed white blouse, khaki slacks, and blue half-inch pump heels.

"I'm so excited," she exclaimed, pouring a cup of coffee. "It's been nearly a year since I've been to Boston."

"You can take Ethan's convertible," Ron said.

"But don't bang it up!" Ethan cried.

"Oh wonderful!" Maggie exclaimed. "The weather is perfect. We can drive with the top down. How would you like that, Charlie?"

"Just fine," Charlie said.

By 10:00 a.m., Charlie and Maggie were whizzing across the Charlestown Bridge, headed for the heart of Boston. Their first stop was Barneys on Huntington, where Charlie picked out a $900 Saint Laurent twill shirt and a $225 pair of James Perse five-pocket pants. Maggie was very encouraging, saying that he needn't worry about the cost.

"It's all on me," she said.

Next, they walked down Newbury Street and stopped in at Riccardi, where Maggie eagerly purchased three pairs of summer shorts for Charlie and a light cotton blouse for herself. In

Loro Piana, Charlie found the perfect pair of elk leather loafers for $915. Maggie picked out a pair of calfskin leather sandals for herself at the bargain price of $995. Their next stop was Alton Lane. Charlie walked out of the store with four gingham button-ups at $125 a pop. They finished up at Hermès, purchasing several sets of short polyester socks and cotton underwear.

All in all, it was a successful shopping spree. Their next stop was the Verizon Wireless store, where Maggie insisted on adding Charlie to the family phone plan. She bought him a brand-new iPhone 6—the latest model—and together they programmed Maggie's, Ron's, and Ethan's numbers into the phone.

"Thank you," Charlie said, relieved that he hadn't had to spend a cent of his measly inheritance.

"It's no problem at all," Maggie insisted. "And after lunch, I was hoping you would run a special errand with me."

"Of course," Charlie said.

They ate at the nearby Atlantic Fish Company before heading east on Route 9.

"One more stop," Maggie said. "Ron doesn't know we're doing this. If he did, he'd throttle me."

"Where are we going?"

"We have an appointment at the Harvard Medical School. Dr. Spritzer set it up for us. He knows a doctor there who should be able to help."

"Help with what?"

"You'll see."

Charlie grew quiet, remembering Maggie's conversations with Dr. Spritzer.

They pulled into the visitor parking lot at the Harvard Medical School, crossed a big lawn on foot, and entered a building called the Department of Neurobiology. Once inside, Maggie pulled out a Post-it note with an address on it and said, "It's room number twenty-four. Should be on the first floor."

Charlie and Maggie wandered up and down the halls for some time. The building was a maze, and nobody was around on a Saturday to help. Finally, they came to the door labeled 24. The placard read "Dr. C. S. Thomas, MD/PhD."

"Here we go," Maggie said, and she knocked.

There was a pause and then the rustle of papers beyond the door. Finally, the door opened, and there stood a middle-aged man, about five foot five, balding, with tufts of brown hair sticking out from both sides of his head.

"I hope we're on time," Maggie said.

"Of course, of course," said the little man. "You must be Maggie. I'm so glad Dr. Spritzer was able to put us in touch."

"And this is Charlie," Maggie said, indicating that Charlie should step forward.

"Nice to meet you, Charlie. I'm Dr. Thomas."

Charlie shook the doctor's hand.

"Please sit down." The office was long and narrow with nothing more than a few wooden chairs, a long desk, a filing cabinet, and a computer. Maggie and Charlie sat in two chairs on one side of the narrow room, and Dr. Thomas sat in a chair facing them.

"So," said Dr. Thomas, looking expectantly at Maggie. "What can I do for you?"

"Well, Dr. Thomas," Maggie began. "I come to you asking for your discretion in this matter. I wouldn't want to attract any…well…*attention*."

"What you say here will be held in the strictest confidence."

"That's very reassuring," Maggie went on. "Let me start by explaining that I wouldn't have come here if I didn't think you could help. You see, Charlie here is a clone."

Charlie sat straight up in his chair. He had no idea this meeting was going to be about *him*.

Dr. Thomas squinted at Charlie as if he couldn't see him properly. "I see," he said. "And what seems to be the problem."

"He doesn't remember everything about his old life. Only certain things. I was wondering if there was any way you could help him."

Charlie sat stunned. This guy was going to think Maggie was off her rocker. Everybody with an ounce of sense knew that clones couldn't *remember* the past. And Dr. Thomas here was going to tell Maggie just that, and the whole ruse would be up. Charlie wouldn't have a chance of convincing Ron and Maggie that he was as good as the original Charles Abernathy Vanderough. He would be exposed for the complete fraud he was.

Dr. Thomas leaned back in the chair and pursed his little mouth.

"So you've had retroactive re-cognition therapy, then, have you?" he said, nodding.

"What?" said Charlie.

"You're not alone," Dr. Thomas continued. "Many clones from the late nineties underwent retroactive re-cognition therapy—as infants. But you wouldn't remember it. You were too young at the time."

"What is retroactive—"

"Retroactive re-cognition therapy. It's a very complicated procedure designed to help clones develop the memories of their donors. However, Marmorkrebs Incorporated and other cloning services stopped the practice about three years ago when manufacturers saw a spike in clinical depression among RRT patients."

"Oh my God," gasped Maggie. "That's terrible."

Dr. Thomas nodded. "Yes, indeed it is. Charlie, have you had any suicidal thoughts?"

"No, sir."

"Tell me, what do you remember?"

Charlie thought of the man in the gray cardigan—the man who turned out to be Franz Vanderough, Charles Abernathy's father. Charlie had seen the man in his dreams before he had seen the portrait of Franz in the Helmsley House library. Perhaps that had been a real memory after all.

"I don't remember much," Charlie said, somewhat sheepishly. He felt as though he had gotten tangled up in his own lies, and he didn't know how much to give away and how much to keep to himself.

"All the better," said Dr. Thomas. "It seems the more successful the retroactive re-cognition therapy is in helping clones develop memories, the more likely they are to have suicidal ideation."

Dr. Thomas turned now to Maggie. "I'm afraid it's better for everybody if Charlie has as few memories as possible. Consider yourselves lucky that he doesn't remember much."

* * *

Maggie was silent the entire drive home. Charlie didn't mind. He was caught up in his own thoughts. *Could he really remember things from Charles Abernathy's past?* That might explain the nightmares he'd been having. But did that mean he'd start to remember more and more the longer he stayed with Ron and Maggie? And then what? Could he really be driven to suicide?

It was hard to swallow. Back at Price-Harold, there had been no talk of memories. No talk of suicide. But then again, Charlie could be a special case. According to Dr. Thomas, not every clone had undergone retroactive re-cognition therapy.

"I was thinking of Mexican food for dinner," Maggie said, breaking the silence.

"Sure."

They drove on for a while longer, and then Maggie said, "You mustn't tell Ron about our visit to Dr. Thomas. Ron doesn't like the idea of my meddling with your memories."

"OK," Charlie said.

"And I suppose we ought to avoid bringing up the past. We don't want to trigger any suicidal thoughts."

"I wouldn't worry too much about that," Charlie said. "I feel fine."

"Nevertheless, you heard what Dr. Thomas said."

"Yes, ma'am."

Charlie wasn't so sure that he agreed with Maggie's plan. In fact, if he really could develop more memories, then what was to stop him from taking over for the original Charles Abernathy Vanderough? He could pick up where the old Charles had left off. And besides, Charlie didn't like being kept in the dark—he wanted to know more about the old Charles and his whacko family. Most importantly, Charlie wanted to stake his claim to the Vanderough fortune.

CHAPTER 16

CHARLIE AWOKE the next morning to the piercing cry of the blue rotary telephone. He groaned and put a pillow over his head.

"Shut up, shut up, shut up," he muttered as the phone rang again.

Finally it stopped. Charlie was on the verge of slipping back into unconsciousness when a loud knock came at his door.

"Yeah," Charlie mumbled. "What is it?"

The door creaked open and there stood Sonia. She hesitated on the threshold, looking about the room like a frightened animal.

"Come in," said Charlie, sitting up in bed.

"Mr. Charlie," Sonia began. "The phone is for you. It is a Mr. Hsiu."

Charlie leaped out of bed and picked up the blue receiver.

"Eric?" he cried into the phone.

Sonia slipped out of the room and closed the door behind her.

"Hey, Charlie!" The voice was Eric's all right. "I found you!"

"Yeah," said Charlie. "How'd you manage that?"

"I just did a search for Vanderough online, and this was the only number that came up."

"Yeah, I'm living with my donor's family in Massachu-setts." And then, not wanting to explain the complicated situation further, Charlie turned the focus onto Eric. "What's new? Where are you calling from?"

"I'm in California."

"Whoa," said Charlie. "That's great!"

"Yeah. My donor set me up in this big house in Westlake. I'm right on the beach, and there's a beautiful golf course right behind me, and I've got a membership now. It's really great! I was calling to see if you wanted to fly out here and join me sometime this summer."

"I'd love to," Charlie said. "But I'm just getting settled here at Helmsley House. Maybe in July or August."

"Whatever works for you," said Eric. "I've got nothing to do but play golf and read on the beach."

"Yeah," said Charlie, trying not to sound envious. "That's cool."

"So what is it like living with your donor's family? Are they cool?"

"It's a little weird. Big house. Lots of nice cars. I just spent like three grand on a new wardrobe."

"Nice!" said Eric.

"Oh, and I just got my own iPhone, so you can reach me at that number anytime you want."

"Awesome, me too."

Charlie and Eric exchanged phone numbers.

"It's really good to hear from you," Charlie said, suddenly feeling very sorry for himself.

"You too."

"Oh Eric! One more thing. Have you ever heard of retro-active re-cognition therapy?"

"No—what's that?"

"Never mind. It's just something stupid I was reading about."

"Cool. Well, text me some photos of your new digs when you get a chance."

"Will do," Charlie said. "Have a good one."

"You too."

And with that, Charlie hung up the phone.

Two minutes later, Charlie's cell phone buzzed. Eric had sent a picture of himself on a broad sandy beach with a big glass house in the background.

Charlie shoved the phone into his pocket and headed downstairs. It was already noon, and Charlie was starving. He found Ron and Maggie in the kitchen. Maggie was sitting at the little table, her eyes glued to the television set above the refrigerator. Ron was reading the *National Review*.

"Good morning," Charlie said.

Maggie unglued her eyes from the television and smiled at Charlie. "Who was that on the phone?" she asked.

"It was an old friend from Price-Harold. He wanted to invite me to his beach house in California."

Maggie's smile vanished. Ron put down the paper.

"Will you be going?" Ron asked gruffly.

Charlie wondered what about Eric's invitation could cause Ron and Maggie so much alarm. Perhaps they would actually miss him if he left.

"I don't think I want to go just now," Charlie said. "I feel like I'm finally settling in here."

Maggie and Ron stared at Charlie in silence.

"That is, unless you want me to go."

Maggie glanced at Ron. Ron seemed to nod. And then Maggie jumped up. "Of course we don't want you to go, Charlie. You can stay here as long as you want."

"OK," said Charlie.

"Good," said Maggie.

"Good," said Ron.

Maggie returned to her seat at the little table and turned her attention to the soap opera on the television. Sonia came in and started sweeping the floors, so Charlie took that as his cue to leave. He grabbed a bagel and exited out the back door.

Ethan was outside, waxing his new Boxster.

"Going for another ride today?" Charlie asked as he came

upon him.

"Naw." Ethan groaned. "Dad won't let me."

Then Charlie had an idea.

"Ethan, can you take a picture of me with your Porsche?"

"What for?"

"I want to show a friend of mine."

"OK," Ethan said. He took Charlie's phone and snapped a few shots of Charlie standing beside the Boxster with the top down.

"Thanks," Charlie said. Then he picked the best photo and sent it off to Eric.

Charlie was bored, so he wandered out to the greenhouse. Abel was there tending to some avocado trees.

"Hola," Charlie ventured.

Abel just nodded and continued to prune the avocado trees.

Charlie wandered into the back shed where he had seen the beautiful Latina woman only days earlier. Still there was no trace of her. Charlie kicked around a bit, looking for a trapdoor. Nothing.

"Adios," Charlie said to Abel as he left.

Abel made no reply.

What was there to do around here on a Sunday? Charlie wondered. It certainly wasn't a beachfront property in California. Charlie's phone buzzed again. This time, Eric was posing with a 9-iron club on a grassy golf course.

From where he stood, Charlie could get a good picture of

the whole of Helmsley House. He ran it through a few filters before sending it off to Eric.

"Creepy," Eric wrote back.

Charlie kicked up the gravel in the drive.

Then Maggie appeared at the back door. "Charlie," she called. "Do you want to come with me into town? I've got some errands to run."

"Sure," Charlie said. He had nothing better to do.

Maggie pulled her SUV out of the carriage house and sidled up next to Charlie. "Hop in," she said.

Together, they took off down the long drive. When they came to the gate, Maggie took a sharp right onto Rolling Hills Way.

"I thought town was the other way," Charlie said.

"It is," Maggie said. "We're not going into town."

"But I thought—"

"Charlie, we lied to you."

Maggie's face was tense. Her eyes remained on the road. Both hands gripped the steering wheel.

Charlie didn't say a thing.

"Ron told you that you died...that...the old Charles died in a car accident."

"Yes," Charlie said. The vision of the young man in the road came flooding back. Maggie playing with the knob on the radio. The sudden swerving. Slamming into the tree. A wave of nausea swept through Charlie. He rolled down the window, thinking he would be sick again.

"Well, that wasn't true," Maggie went on.

The more Maggie talked, the sicker Charlie felt. He didn't want her to go on. The memory was too visceral.

"You survived the crash," Maggie said.

Maggie suddenly came to an abrupt stop. And there it was. That goddamned tree with the scarred bark. The mangled fence. Charlie leaned out of the window and vomited.

"Charlie!" Maggie cried. "Oh Charlie! Are you carsick?"

Charlie opened the car door and leaned over on the pavement, trying to catch his breath. Bile rose in his throat.

Maggie jumped out of the car, came around, and put her hand on Charlie's back.

"It's OK, honey. It's OK." She rubbed his back gently. Familiarly. As if she had known Charlie for years.

When the nausea finally passed, Charlie found a flat patch of grass on the side of the road and sat down.

"You just sit," Maggie said. "Relax."

Maggie sat beside him and stroked his back.

"I'm sorry we lied to you. The crash. It happened here. Do you remember?"

Charlie nodded.

"We were in the car together," Maggie said. "Do you remember that?"

"Yes."

"And you swerved to avoid a deer."

Charlie looked at Maggie. That made more sense. The young man in the gray cardigan. If that had been Franz Vanderough, as Charlie suspected it was, then it couldn't have been him in the middle of the road. The Franz he remembered, the Franz from the portrait, had been too young. The original Charles wouldn't have been born yet. Charlie must have confused two different memories: the memory of the crash and the memory of the portrait in the library.

Still—something didn't make sense.

"Why were we in the car together?" Charlie asked.

"That doesn't matter," Maggie said. "Best not to go into it. Remember what Dr. Thomas said. It's better that you don't remember some things."

"Then why are you telling me all this now?" Charlie asked. "Why not let me go on thinking I died in a car crash?"

"Because the way you died was much worse," Maggie said. Tears flooded her eyes. "And I think you need to know."

"OK then," Charlie said, "How did I die?"

"You killed yourself," Maggie blurted. Tears streamed freely down her face. "You killed yourself, and I'm so scared you're going to do it again."

Now it was Charlie's turn to comfort Maggie. He put his hand on her shoulder.

"It was awful," Maggie said. "Nobody saw it coming. You seemed fine. And then—"

Maggie trailed off. Charlie felt sick again.

"I'm confused," Charlie said. "I thought Franz killed himself."

Maggie started bawling. "Yes, yes. He did. He did."

"So you're saying Franz and Charles both committed suicide."

"Yes," Maggie cried. "It runs in the family. And I'm afraid you're going to do it again. After what Dr. Thomas said—"

"But Maggie," Charlie said, "I feel fine."

"Do you? Do you? That's what the old Charles said right before he killed himself."

"Maggie," Charlie said. "Really, I feel OK."

But Charlie didn't feel OK. The more they talked about the past, the sicker he felt. Still, Charlie wanted to know more.

"How did I kill myself?" Charlie asked.

"You shot yourself in the head. You used the same pistol your father used to kill himself."

Charlie sat in silence, fighting back the urge to vomit.

"What about the car crash?" Charlie asked. "Were we hurt?"

Maggie nodded.

"How badly?"

"You were in the hospital for six months. That's why you dropped out of Yale. The accident happened when you were home for spring break. We were both on spring break. And after the accident, you didn't go back to school."

"What about you?" Charlie asked. "Were you hurt?"

"I was in a wheelchair for a year. Yes."

"And then how long was it until I killed myself?" Charlie asked.

"I don't know. Fourteen, maybe fifteen years."

Charlie and Maggie sat in silence for some time. Charlie's hand lingered on Maggie's shoulder. Something in him felt close to her. Closer than he had felt to anyone in his whole life. It confused Charlie. Then again, he and Maggie had suffered a serious trauma together. It was no wonder he felt connected to her in some strange way.

"Let's go home," Charlie said. "I don't think it's good for either of us to be here."

Charlie looked at the scarred tree and felt the bile rise in his throat again.

"OK, Charlie. OK." Maggie rose and took a few slow steps toward the car. Then she turned to face Charlie again. "Just promise me you won't kill yourself again."

"I promise," Charlie said.

They drove back in silence. Maggie put her plump hand on Charlie's knee and kept it there for the whole drive. Charlie felt oddly comforted by the gesture.

As they pulled up the long drive to the carriage house, Maggie said, "Please don't tell Ron about this. He didn't want me to tell you. Your suicide—it's too hard for him to talk about."

"Yes," said Charlie. "I understand."

Ron was in the exact same place at the little table reading the paper when they came in through the back door.

"Back so soon," he said without looking up.

"I forgot my wallet," Maggie lied.

"Hmm." Ron nodded.

* * *

That night, Maggie skipped dinner. Ron didn't seem to think anything of it.

"Menopause," he said to Charlie as they all sat down to a meal of ribs and potato salad that Ron had ordered in from a local barbeque.

After dinner, Ethan convinced Ron to let him practice driving in the dark. The two of them clambered into the Porsche Boxster and took off down the drive. Mamma Beth retired to her bedroom, where she turned the radio on full blast. And Charlie closed himself up in his room, drawing the curtains around the canopy bed, and fell asleep.

CHAPTER 17

IN THE MIDDLE OF THE NIGHT, Charlie awoke to the sounds of footsteps on the wooden floor just beyond the curtains of his canopy bed. He lay there, thinking at first he must have dreamed them. The room was eerily quiet, and the house lay in deep silence. Charlie waited, listening for the sound to come again. The only thing he could hear was the hiss of his own labored breath.

Charlie clutched the sheets to his chest and lay perfectly still.

Then it came again. Four solid beats. *Thump. Thump. Thump. Thump.*

Somebody was coming toward Charlie just on the other side of the curtain.

Charlie froze. He wanted to cry out, to say anything, but the darkness seemed to suffocate him.

Suddenly, the curtain flung open, and there stood the imposing figure of the woman from the greenhouse—wide hips, broad shoulders, round brown eyes, soft red lips, and one long dark braid down her back. She was naked now too, and Charlie could trace the faint trail of dark pubic hair from her naval to her genitalia.

The woman's face was masked in shadow, but the whites of her teeth and eyes burned through the darkness.

Charlie cowered. He tried to think of something to say.

Then the woman turned and walked to the door. She looked back over her shoulder as if to say, "Follow me," then exited the room.

Charlie leaped to his feet. He noticed that he had become aroused. This strange woman frightened and excited him. He followed her into the hall, where she now stood in front of the door Charlie had been unable to open a few days before. She tried the handle, and the door swung outward. Then the woman disappeared inside.

Fearful he might lose her again, Charlie rushed to the door. A darkened stairwell led the way up into the topmost chamber of the house. Charlie climbed slowly. The woman was nowhere to be seen.

Charlie emerged in a dark attic. The shadow of the woman loomed beyond Charlie's reach. There was a light switch on the wall, and Charlie flicked it instinctively. The lights came on, and the woman seemed to melt away. In her place stood a sewing mannequin amid stacks of boxes and bags.

Was he dreaming? Where had she come from? Where had

she gone?

Charlie sniffed about the attic. There was no place the woman could have gone. Was he going mad?

Then something caught his eye. Lying face up on the top of a box was a picture mounted in a black oak frame. In the photo, a man and woman stood face-to-face, hand in hand. The woman wore a white wedding dress and veil; the man donned a black suit. Charlie couldn't believe his eyes. The bride in the photo was a much younger, thinner Maggie. She looked no more than twenty years old. And the groom—Charlie felt a wave of nausea again—the groom was Charlie.

Charlie tore into the box. It was filled with photos of Charles Abernathy Vanderough as a young man—looking exactly like Charlie looked now. And Maggie was there too. *His wife.*

Suddenly, things started to make sense. Maggie's frequent tears. Ron's nervous manner. They were afraid Charlie would suddenly remember that he had once been married to Maggie.

That explained why the house had been left in Maggie's name and not Ron's. Maggie was the heir to the Vanderough estate!

Charlie thumbed through photo after photo. There were a few of Ron and another woman. An old girlfriend maybe—or an ex-wife.

As he picked his way through the pile of old photographs, Charlie began to hatch a plan. If he had once been Maggie's husband, then what was to stop him from winning her back and staking his claim on the Vanderough fortune once and for all? Ron had no right to it. That interloper! That cheat! That scoundrel! Surely Maggie would feel as though she owed Charlie something, especially if he could reignite the old spark from their past.

Yes! That was how Charlie was going to get his money back.

Charlie put the photos back in the box and crept back to bed. He slept soundly for the rest of the night.

CHAPTER 18

"**G**OOD MORNING, ETHAN.**" Charlie entered the kitchen bright and early. "It's summer break for you, isn't it? What have you got going on today?"

"I dunno," Ethan said into a bowl of cereal.

"Good morning, Ron." Charlie continued.

"Good morning, Charlie. You seem chipper."

"Yes, I got an excellent night's sleep." Charlie walked up to Maggie, who was heating oatmeal on the stovetop. He leaned in and kissed her on the cheek.

Maggie turned bright red.

"You *do* seem to be in a good mood today," Maggie said. "I'm so glad."

"Anyone interested in a picnic?" Charlie asked. "I was thinking we could eat outside today."

"I'm busy," Ethan said, getting up from the table.

"I have to go into work," Ron grumbled.

"Then I guess it'll be just you and me, Maggie."

Charlie smiled, and Maggie blushed again.

That afternoon, Charlie made two turkey sandwiches, threw together a mixed salad, and grabbed a bottle of wine for his picnic with Maggie. Together, they walked out onto the big lawn and unfurled a blanket in the shade of the willow tree.

"What a nice idea," Maggie said as she unwrapped her sandwich. "Ron would never think to have a picnic."

Charlie uncorked the Merlot and poured a full glass for Maggie and then one for himself.

"Cheers," he said. And their glasses clinked.

"I'm sorry about yesterday," Maggie said, her face red. "I just had to make sure you weren't going to kill yourself again. It was too painful to go through once. You can understand why I brought it up the way I did, can't you?"

"Don't you worry about it, Mags," Charlie said.

Maggie blushed again.

"Nobody has called me Mags since Charles died."

Charlie reached over and put his hand on top of Maggie's. She didn't pull it away. Instead, they just sat there for a while, not looking at each other, fingers touching.

"How long do you think you'll stay with us?" Maggie asked after some time.

"As long as you'll have me," Charlie said. He stared into her eyes. She looked away.

"Do you like it here?" Maggie asked. "Are you happy with

us?"

"It feels like I've come home," Charlie said. "I can't explain it—the more time we spend together, the more I feel like I've known you my whole life."

"Do you remember me now?" Maggie asked, pulling her hand from Charlie's.

"I seem to remember that you were a very important part of my life," Charlie said.

"Oh Charles!" Maggie exclaimed.

"I think I must have loved you," Charlie said.

Maggie started sobbing. She buried her face in her hands. Her glass of wine tipped over in the grass.

"I loved you too," she exclaimed. "Oh Charlie. I can't keep it from you any longer. Surely you remember! We were married."

Charlie seized the moment and kissed Maggie full on the lips.

When they both looked up, Abel was in the drive staring at them.

"Oh no!" Maggie cried. "No, no, no. What are we doing?"

She leaped up and ran across the lawn and into the house, leaving Charlie under the willow tree.

Abel said nothing and headed out toward the greenhouse.

Maggie didn't leave her room for three days. Charlie had to content himself roaming about the big house, reading books in the library, or playing billiards in the den. Ron made excuses for Maggie, claiming she was sick. Sonia brought her chicken soup and hot water bottles to warm the bed, even though it was ninety degrees outside.

Charlie knew she wasn't sick, at least not with the flu. Clearly, she was embarrassed by what had happened. It was a very complicated situation, and Charlie wanted to give Maggie room to work it out in her head. He'd be ready when she reemerged.

And she did reemerge. It was a Thursday. Ron was at work, and Ethan was off rock climbing with some friends. Sonia and Abel had the day off, so the only people in the house were Charlie, Maggie, and Mamma Beth.

Charlie was sitting at the little table in the kitchen watching *Wake Up, Boston!* when Maggie appeared in the hall. She tightened the sash on her bathrobe and stepped into the kitchen.

"Charlie," she said.

Charlie waited. Maggie stood with her hands at her sides—she looked exhausted.

"Charlie, I don't know what to do."

Charlie stood and went to her. He put his hand on her shoulder.

"Don't you worry, Mags," he said. "I'm here now. We're together. Nothing can hurt you now."

Maggie collapsed into Charlie's arms and buried her face in his shoulder.

"I've missed you so much," she said.

"Shh." Charlie soothed. "Let's get you back into bed."

Charlie led Maggie up the stairs and into the primary bedroom suite. Once inside, he pulled back the blankets on the bed and invited Maggie to lie down.

Maggie obeyed.

Charlie began to undress. He had been with a woman only once before. Charlie and some other boys from Price-Harold had snuck out one night and had taken the train into New York City where they drank and smoked and made fools of themselves. And then they met Lady Rose, who invited them into her brothel. Charlie paid $200 to spend an hour with a buxom woman named Florette. She had been kind and gentle and had guided Charlie through all the motions of making love.

Now Charlie stood before Maggie, exposed, his member growing stiff as Maggie looked on. Maggie untied her sash and spread the robe open, revealing two large, round breasts. She was rotund, Rubenesque, like the women in old Flemish paintings. Charlie found himself aroused by the soft, supple contours of her body.

Charlie climbed into the bed and started kissing Maggie's neck. She closed her eyes and let him take control.

When they had finished, Charlie lay on the bed beside her and held her in his arms. She was crying.

Then Maggie fell asleep. Charlie rose and bundled his clothes in his arms and climbed upstairs to his bedroom. He plopped himself down on his bed and waited.

CHAPTER 19

MAGGIE WAS LOOKING SPRITELY Friday morning. She flitted about the kitchen, making eggs and bacon and toast for Ron, Ethan, and Charlie.

Ron looked pensive. A few times, Charlie looked up from his breakfast to find Ron staring intently in his direction. It made Charlie uncomfortable, but he played it off, asking Ron a barrage of questions.

"Do you have an office you go to?" Charlie asked.

"Yes," grumbled Ron.

"And do other people help you manage the estate?"

"No."

"You don't have a lawyer?"

"Hm," said Ron, chewing his bacon. "A lawyer. Well, yes. When we need one."

"Who's your lawyer?"

Ron slammed his fists down on the table.

"What's with the third degree? Can't I just eat my breakfast in peace?"

Maggie rushed over and poured some more coffee into Ron's mug.

"Don't get angry, dear," she said. "Charlie just wants to know more about the family business. Remember that Charles wanted Charlie to help you manage the estate someday."

"Well we don't have to start this morning, do we? All this talk is giving me a headache."

Maggie left the room and returned with a bottle of aspirin. She placed it in front of Ron.

Ethan excused himself from the table and skulked away to do God knows what. Ron popped a few aspirin into his mouth and ordered Maggie to turn on the TV. Maggie flicked the switch on the television set and sat down to eat her own breakfast. Charlie could feel her slippered foot touching his under the table.

"Isn't Sonia coming in today?" Ron asked after some time. "She's late."

"I don't know," Maggie said. "She should be here by now. I haven't seen Abel's truck."

They sat in silence a while longer until finally Ron said, "I'm going to work. I'll see you tonight."

Ron pulled his Porsche out of the carriage house and took off down the long drive.

Suddenly, Maggie launched herself onto Charlie, kissing his ears and neck and shoulders. Charlie pushed her back gently and hissed, "Where's Ethan? He's still here, isn't he?"

"We can go to my room," Maggie whispered. "He won't even think to bother us until lunch."

Then the phone rang. Maggie gave an exasperated sigh and left to take the call in the den. When she returned, she looked glum.

"That was Ron," she said. "He just found Abel and Sonia on the side of the road. Abel's truck broke down, and Ron is calling Triple-A to come and tow the truck into town. He says we have to go out there and pick up Sonia. She still wants to come in to work today. I suspect she needs the money."

"OK," Charlie said. "A little adventure together."

Maggie's smile returned to her face. "Like we used to do!" she said. "We used to drive all over the state."

Maggie backed the SUV out of the carriage house, and Charlie hopped in. Throughout the drive, Maggie's hand was on Charlie's knee.

About three miles out, they came upon Ron and Abel and the tow truck. Sonia was standing on the side of the road, while Ron and Abel helped the man from Triple-A attach Abel's old pickup to the rig.

"Get in, Sonia," Maggie said as they pulled up alongside her.

Sonia obeyed and climbed into the seat right behind Charlie.

"Thank you, Mrs. Vanderough," she said. "I appreciate you coming all the way out here to get me."

"Oh, I know you need the work," Maggie said. "It was no trouble at all."

Sonia blushed.

"How have you been, Sonia?" Maggie went on. "Are you still seeing that fellow from your salsa class."

"No, ma'am," Sonia said.

"Have you met any other nice boys?"

"No, ma'am. There aren't many men my father would approve of here in Amherst."

"That's a shame," Maggie said.

It was Charlie's turn to ask a question.

"Sonia, your family has been working at Helmsley House for decades, am I right?"

"Yes, sir."

"And you grew up helping your mom around the house."

"Yes."

"Do you happen to have any pictures of her?"

"Not with me. But I can bring a picture one of these days, if you like."

Charlie nodded. "That would be nice. I would love to see your mother."

* * *

Charlie and Maggie spent the rest of the morning wandering the grounds of Helmsley Park as Sonia cleaned the house. They explored the greenhouse together, and Charlie was surprised to learn that Maggie hadn't been in the greenhouse in decades.

"I never come out here," Maggie said as they examined the ripening avocados on the avocado tree.

Charlie came up behind Maggie and kissed her neck.

"Not here!" Maggie hissed. "This place is haunted."

"Why do you say that?" Charlie asked.

"It's just something Charles always said."

"I wonder why he would say that?"

"You would know better than anyone," Maggie said, poking Charlie in the side playfully. "Do you remember why you always said this place was haunted?"

Charlie shook his head.

"Dr. Spritzer says I'm gullible," Maggie went on. "He says I'll believe anything."

Charlie touched Maggie's arm.

"I know you've been going to see Dr. Spritzer," he ventured. "Is everything OK?"

Maggie hugged herself and looked away. Charlie could see tears forming in her eyes.

"If you don't want to talk about it—"

"No. No. It's OK," Maggie said, wiping the tears from her eyes.

"Are you OK?" Charlie asked again.

Maggie looked Charlie straight in the eye. "How could I be OK? You've come back from the dead. I'm married to your brother now. But I love you. It's a mess!"

"But Dr. Spritzer—" Charlie began.

"Dr. Spritzer warned me that this could happen. He said I should be careful about getting too close to you. He said it could awaken old feelings."

"So Dr. Spritzer is your—"

"Therapist. Well, really he's a psychiatrist. He prescribes my antianxiety medication. I have an anxiety disorder. Although Ron refuses to believe in such things."

Charlie nodded.

"So you're not dying?"

Maggie laughed. "How sweet of you to worry about me. You darling boy. I love you so much."

Maggie leaned in and kissed Charlie full on the lips.

They were just leaving the greenhouse when they heard a cry from the house.

"Missus! Missus!"

Sonia burst from the house and waved her arms wildly in the air.

"Missus! Mamma Beth has fallen down the stairs."

Maggie gulped and took off running toward the house. Charlie followed close behind. When they got inside, they found Mamma Beth lying at the bottom of the stairs in the fetal position. She was conscious, but she was speaking babble.

"Call nine one one!" Maggie cried.

Charlie ran to the phone and ordered an ambulance to come to the house.

"Don't you worry, Mamma Beth," Maggie cooed. "Help is on the way."

Mamma Beth squirmed on the floor, crying.

"Twenty-three, forty-two, seventeen!" she whined. "Twenty-three, forty-two, seventeen!"

"What's she saying?" Sonia asked.

"It sounds like she's counting. Mamma Beth, are you counting?"

"Twenty-three, forty-two, seventeen."

"She must have hit her head," Sonia said. "She has a lump."

"Yes," Maggie said. "I see it."

"What was she doing up?" Charlie asked.

"She said she wanted to get something out of the den," Sonia explained. "I didn't think anything of it. Then I heard the fall."

"The ambulance is here," Charlie said.

Two paramedics came through the front door carrying a stretcher. They examined Mamma Beth and determined she had a concussion. They advised taking her to the hospital for overnight monitoring.

"Whatever you say," Maggie said. "You can take her in the ambulance, and we'll follow you in the car."

Sonia stayed back at the house. Charlie and Maggie climbed into Maggie's SUV, and they followed the ambulance to the hospital.

"You'd better call Ron," Maggie said to Charlie.

Charlie pulled out his cell phone and dialed Ron's number. There was no answer, so Charlie left a hurried message explaining what had happened.

They reached town in ten minutes. They zoomed by the university and past Ming Chen's Chinese Restaurant. Then they turned down Arlington and passed the Porsche dealership. Charlie pointed.

"Isn't that Ron? At the dealership."

Maggie looked. "Yes."

"I'll try calling him again," Charlie said. This time Ron picked up. He agreed to meet them both at the hospital.

Mamma Beth was checked into a private room. A nurse took her vitals and confirmed that she was doing OK, just a little woozy. The doctor performed a full examination and seconded the paramedics' prognosis: Mamma Beth had a minor concussion. Because of her age and the state of her mind, the doctor wanted to monitor Mamma Beth for twenty-four hours to see if there were any further developments.

Mamma Beth had found the remote control for the little television set mounted on the wall and was already watching TV by the time the doctor left them alone in her room.

Ron looked worried. "I want to stay with her tonight," he said.

"I'll stay with you," Maggie said.

"No, no. Ethan will need looking after. And Sonia still needs a ride home. You and Charlie should head back and take care of things around the house. I'll be fine here tonight."

Maggie agreed. She and Charlie drove back to the house in silence.

Ethan had been down the road at a neighbor's house when Mamma Beth had fallen. He was waiting for them when they got home.

"Sonia told me what happened," he said. "Is Grandma all right?"

"She'll be fine," Maggie assured him. "What do you want for dinner? I'll pick something up after I take Sonia home. Sonia, are you ready to go?"

Maggie took off with Sonia, leaving Ethan and Charlie sitting at the kitchen table.

"How old are you?" Ethan asked after some time.

"Eighteen," Charlie said.

"What's the deal with you and my mother?" he asked.

Charlie's heart thumped.

"What do you mean?"

"You two are hanging out all the time. She's, like, thirty years older than you. I don't get it."

"Your mother is a very interesting woman," Charlie said. "And she's been very kind to me."

"How long are you planning to stay?" Ethan asked. "I thought you were going to find your own place."

"Why? Am I bothering you?"

Ethan shrugged. Then he dug his phone out of his pocket and started texting. Charlie took that as his cue to head up to his room.

* * *

Late that night, when he was certain Ethan had gone to bed, Charlie crept down to the second-floor primary bedroom and opened the door. Maggie was there with the lamp on, reading in bed. She smiled when Charlie came in.

"Shh." She hissed. "Shut the door, quick!"

Charlie closed the door behind him and tiptoed over to Maggie's bedside.

"I've been thinking about you all evening," he said.

"And I you."

Charlie climbed into the bed with Maggie and pressed his head into her bosom.

"Tell me about our wedding," he said.

"It wasn't long after the car accident. You had just gotten out of the hospital, and I was still in a wheelchair. And you proposed to me at Ming Chen's."

"At Ming Chen's?"

"Yes, it was where we went on our first date in our junior year of high school."

"We were high-school sweethearts?"

"Yes, we were. And we were very much in love." Maggie shifted so she could look at Charlie's face. "After the accident, you said you didn't want to waste another minute. So you dropped out of Yale, I dropped out of Amherst, and we got married the minute I was well enough to walk down the aisle."

"What was the wedding like?"

"Oh, it was a huge affair. Mamma Beth wouldn't have it any other way. She adored me back then. We were close, Mamma Beth and I, up until I married your brother. She hardly spoke to me after that."

"Do you think she would be happy if she knew we were together again?"

Maggie sighed. "I think Mamma Beth is happy only when she's got her radio on."

Charlie pulled Maggie close.

"Maybe we could have another wedding?" he cooed in her ear.

Maggie whispered, "I would like that. I would like that very much."

* * *

In the middle of the night, Charlie awoke from a bad dream. In it, Mamma Beth had appeared bloody and bruised, crying out, "Twenty-three, forty-two, seventeen." Charlie turned over in the bed. Maggie was curled up next to him, snoring gently. Her eyelids fluttered a bit when Charlie rose, but she did not wake. Charlie put on his clothes in the darkness and then left Maggie sleeping soundly.

He crept downstairs. Mamma Beth was going to get something from the den when she fell down the stairs. Charlie was pretty sure he knew where she had been headed.

He entered the den and walked slowly toward the portrait of Winston Churchill. Charlie removed the portrait and squinted to see the little numbers on the dial of the safe.

He turned the dial carefully. Twenty-three, forty-two, seventeen.

The lock clicked, and the safe swung open.

Charlie peered into the hollow chamber. There was a small package, wrapped in a white towel—the same package Charlie had seen Ron deposit there the previous week.

Charlie reached in. The package was heavy, solid. He unwrapped the cloth carefully.

It was a gun.

Suddenly, Charlie felt nauseous. He dropped the gun back in the safe and ran to the bathroom. Flashes of the gun came flooding back to him. The head of the pistol in his mouth. A click as he pulled the trigger. A loud bang.

Charlie vomited into the toilet.

It was the same gun Charles Abernathy Vanderough had used to kill himself nineteen years ago. Charlie was sure of it. And it was the same gun Charles's father had used to end his life before that.

Charlie waited for the nausea to subside before returning to the safe. There was no telling what Ron would do when he found out about Charlie and Maggie's relationship. Would Ron go into a jealous rage? Would he use the gun to seek his revenge? Charlie grew anxious. Surely Ron would not take the news of Charlie and Maggie quietly. This gun posed a threat to both of them.

And then there was Mamma Beth. She had been on her way to open the safe. There was no telling what she might have done if she had gotten her hands on the pistol.

Charlie withdrew the gun from the safe, fighting the urge to throw up. He closed the safe door, spun the lock, and re-placed the Churchill portrait. Then he wrapped the gun in its cloth and carried it upstairs to his room where he deposited it under his pillow.

CHAPTER 20

IT WOULD TAKE TIME for Maggie to get a divorce, Charlie thought. And who knew how much of the estate she would lose in the proceedings. Nevertheless, Charlie was sure it was the best course of action. Maggie, of course, begged Charlie to hold off telling Ron about their affair. She was still afraid he would strangle them both. Charlie agreed. They needn't say anything right away. But sooner or later, Ron would have to know.

Days went by. Charlie and Maggie carried out their affair in every secret nook and cranny of the big old house. If Ethan knew anything about the affair, then he didn't let on. He spent most of his afternoons out of the house anyway. As for Sonia and Abel, Charlie was pretty sure they both had a solid grasp of the situation, but neither of them was going to say anything to anyone about it.

Then one morning, Maggie came to Charlie looking very

grim. They went for one of their walks around the park, and Maggie said, "Charlie, I need to ask you for help."

"Yes, Mags. What is it?"

"Well, it seems Ron and I have gotten ourselves into a pickle."

"What happened?"

Maggie looked away.

"What is it, Maggie?" Charlie said soothingly.

"I'm afraid I need to ask you for money."

"Money?" Charlie said. "Why would you need money?"

"Charlie, you don't understand, do you?"

"I most certainly do not," Charlie said, a shadow crossing his face.

"Oh Charlie!" Maggie began to cry. "When Charles died, he didn't leave me anything except this big old house. We're cash poor."

"What about Ron?" Charlie demanded. "What about the investments he's been managing?"

"Charlie, there were never any investments."

"But—"

"We lied to you. We wanted to impress you. We thought it was the only way to make you stay with us."

Charlie froze. He couldn't believe what he was hearing.

"What has Ron been doing all day, then?" Charlie demanded.

"He's a car salesman at Amherst Porsche on Arlington Avenue. That day you saw him at the dealership, the day Mamma

Beth hit her head, he wasn't looking at cars. He was selling them."

"If you don't have any money," Charlie interrupted, "then how can you afford all those cars?"

"The cars are leases. We don't own them. Ron gets a good deal from the dealership."

"What about the clothes you bought me?"

"Oh Charlie. We wanted so badly to impress you—"

"Explain to me how you could afford to pay a thousand dollars for a pair of shoes!"

Maggie sighed. "You may have noticed that some of the furniture has gone missing over the last few weeks. Ron has been auctioning off our most valuable possessions. Like the watercolor in the parlor. We got a good deal on that."

"That's got to be worth something. Don't tell me you spent it all already."

"We have. We put it toward our mortgage. You see, some years ago, Ron and I took out a second mortgage on the house. And now we've reached a point where we can't afford to pay the installments anymore. That's where you come in."

"What?"

"Ron had this plan. Well, the idea was mine to begin with. We thought that if we made you a part of the family…you know…took you in, we had hoped you might be willing to help us out—*financially*."

"You had a plan?" Charlie cried.

"Don't yell. Charlie, please don't yell at me. I didn't know that you and I would fall in love. And now I'm earnestly asking for your help. You know the truth now. We need two million dollars to bail us out of the debt we're in."

Charlie wanted to strike Maggie. He clenched his fists and clamped his jaw.

"Well, so much for that plan, then," he said.

"You won't help us?"

"I don't have any money, Maggie."

"But Charles must have left you something. He was worth half a billion at least. I always wondered where his money had gone after he died—since he didn't leave it to me. So when you showed up, I naturally assumed he left all his money to you."

"I hardly got a penny of it," said Charlie. He almost wanted to laugh. "I assumed Charles left all his money to you. That's why I came here in the first place. I thought I could track down the family fortune."

"If Charles didn't leave his money with either of us," Maggie went on, "then where did five hundred million dollars go?"

"I have no idea. But I sure as hell don't have it."

"Oh Charlie," Maggie cried. "What are we going to do?"

"*We* aren't going to do anything! I'm sorry, but it looks like the joke's on both of us."

Maggie stared at Charlie in disbelief.

"But I thought we were going to run away together."

"That was when I thought you were worth millions," Charlie said flatly. "There's no point now."

Maggie collapsed to her knees and started to sob.

Charlie looked at her disdainfully and then tromped back to the house.

CHAPTER 21

"CHARLIE!" ERIC CALLED OUT as Charlie descended the stairs, heading toward the baggage claim.

Charlie was relieved to see a friendly face. He shouldered his bag and extended his hand. Eric swatted the hand away and leaned in for a firm embrace.

"It's so good to see you, Charlie B," Eric said. "I've been a bit lonely this summer out here in California all by myself."

"At least you have your donor," Charlie said.

"Yeah. He's great. He really set me up. But I don't see much of him. He's busy running his company."

"And what do you do all day?"

"I've been hanging out at the beach. Doing some golfing."

"Sounds awful," Charlie joked.

"It can get old. But I'm not complaining. Besides, I start my internship at the company on Monday. My donor wants me to work my way up the corporate ladder and maybe take over for him someday."

"Work? You *want* to work?"

"What else is there to do?" Eric shrugged.

"I dunno. Travel. Shop. Enjoy life!"

"That gets old fast, Charlie." Eric smirked. "Come on, my driver is waiting for us."

Once outside, Charlie and Eric climbed into the back of a black luxury sedan. The driver was a Black man in his mid-forties named Michael.

"Where are we headed, Mr. Eric?" he asked as they buckled their seat belts.

"Let's go home," Eric said. "I want to show Charlie the house."

"It's a fine house." Michael nodded, looking at them through his rearview mirror.

For the duration of the drive, Eric shared everything that had happened to him since his graduation from Price-Harold. He had picked up his file from Headmistress Fruth and had discovered that the original Eric Hsiu had given him several million in stocks and bonds, a beautiful beach house in Westlake, and the opportunity to work at his billion-dollar company, Meta-Haiku. Eric had flown straight to California, where he was greeted by his personal driver, Michael, and taken to the corporate offices of Meta-Haiku, where he met his donor, the original Eric Hsiu.

The meeting had been warm and pleasant for both parties. Eric Sr. was in his midsixties and, except for the white hair and age spots, looked just like Eric B.

Eric B got a tour of the Meta-Haiku campus, which took up all four stories of a brand-new building in Mountain View. The corporate headquarters boasted an expansive cafeteria, several juice bars, a rec room complete with ping-pong, foosball, and air hockey, an old-school video game arcade, a screening room, yoga classes, and two full-size basketball courts—all for employee use at no cost.

To Charlie, it sounded more like a college dormitory than a place of business.

"That's the point," Eric said.

Then Eric pressed Charlie for more information about his experience at Helmsley Park. Charlie, not wanting to reveal that he had been left with nothing, kept his answers purposefully short and vague. Eric still had the impression that Charlie owned Helmsley Park...and a Porsche, and millions of dollars in stocks and bonds—just like he did. Charlie said nothing to persuade Eric otherwise.

* * *

When they pulled up in front of the big glass house where Eric lived, Charlie couldn't help but let out a gasp of amazement. The mansion towered three stories over a broad sandy beach. The green of the adjacent golf course stretched north as far as the eye could see. From the front porch, Charlie could hear the steady *crash-crash* of waves on the beach and the plaintive cries of gulls overhead.

Eric showed Charlie to his room on the second floor. It was big and airy. Several tall glass windows let in the afternoon light. A set of glass doors led out to a private patio overlooking the beach below and the ocean beyond.

As far as Charlie was concerned, this was paradise. He couldn't help but feel a twinge of envy. Charlie barely had enough money in the bank to survive the year, and here was Eric with his grand house on the beach and his membership to an exclusive golf club and his internship at one of the swankiest companies in the world. What would Eric think if he knew Charlie was worth diddly-squat?

Charlie took some time to freshen up after his long journey, and then he and Eric were off for eighteen holes of golf at the Olympic Club next door. Charlie was a pro at golf thanks to many years of training at Price-Harold. But Eric was truly expert. They traversed the course, recalling their time at Price-Harold and wondering what had become of their many friends.

"Donny B should be graduating about now," Eric said. "I wonder if he'll go into the family business."

"Which one?" Charlie joked.

Eric chuckled.

"What about you?" Charlie asked. "Are you looking forward to working for your donor?"

"Well, I'm not working for him directly," Eric said. "I'm interning for a guy named Brian Glazier. He's supposed to be the vice president of marketing or something."

"Have you met him yet?"

"Yeah," Eric said. "Nice guy. Really good at ping-pong."

Then, after a moment's thought, Eric said, "Hey, I have an idea. Why don't you join me for lunch on Monday? I can show you around the office. Plus, the food is great."

"Can I do that?"

"Sure! I'll just have to call in a guest pass for you, and we can have lunch at the cafeteria. Maybe meet my boss."

"Will your donor be there?"

"No. He's in China this week on business."

"I'd love to see it," Charlie said. "Maybe I'll want to work there too."

Eric laughed, but Charlie was half-serious. He would need a job in the coming months if he wanted to survive. He couldn't stay with Eric forever.

CHAPTER 22

MONDAY MORNING, Brian Glazier swiped his card at the front entrance to Meta-Haiku corporate headquarters.

"Hold the door!"

It was Miles, the intern down at digital sales. Brian recognized him by his scruffy beard and unkempt hair. Miles was carrying a long, black gym bag that seemed to be causing him trouble as he shuffled up the steps to where Brian stood holding the door open.

Miles brushed past Brian without a thank-you and hurried down the hall to the stairwell, where he disappeared from view.

CHAPTER 23

ERIC'S DRIVER, MICHAEL, picked Charlie up at 11:30
a.m. on Monday to take him to meet Eric at Meta-Haiku
headquarters. When Charlie got out of the car, he tipped Michael forty dollars and crossed the narrow plaza to where the
Meta-Haiku building stood towering over the neighboring
businesses. A large Alexander Calder sculpture cast a long
shadow across the plaza, and a small rectangular reflecting
pool mirrored the blue sky above.

Eric was waiting for Charlie at the front entrance with a
visitor's pass, and together they went through the slick glass
doors and took the elevator up to Eric's floor. When the elevator doors slid open, Charlie came face-to-face with a
woman on a skateboard.

"Excuse me," the woman said, hopping off the skateboard
and changing places with Charlie in the elevator.

"Come on," Eric said. "I want to show you my office."

Charlie followed Eric down the hall where several men and women were engaged in a paper airplane contest.

"How does anybody get any work done around here?" Charlie asked in a whisper.

"I have no idea," Eric said. "It's my first day, remember?"

They turned a corner and entered a large room cluttered with sofas and recliners. A man snored heavily from one of the La-Z-Boys.

"This is the nap room," Eric whispered.

"This is awesome," said Charlie.

Finally, they came to an array of cubicles, the first of which belonged to Eric.

"This is where I work," Eric said. "Brian's office is right across the hall." He pointed to a glass corner office where two men were watching YouTube videos of dogs chasing their tales. Charlie could read their names on the placards outside the door: Brian Glazier and Grayson McDougal.

"Which one is your boss?" Charlie asked.

"The one with the red hair."

"Who's the other guy?"

"He's the head of the advertising team."

"Hmm," said Charlie, wondering if the head of the advertising team needed an intern. "Are you going to introduce me?"

"Sure," said Eric, crossing the hallway.

He knocked on the glass door, and Brian Glazier yelled, "Come in!" without even looking up from the computer.

Eric and Charlie entered.

"Come and watch this," Brian commanded. They all gathered around his computer to watch a video of a dog running in circles until it threw up. Brian and Grayson burst out laughing. Eric and Charlie followed suit and chuckled politely.

"Brian," said Eric once the video had stopped, "this is my friend Charlie from school. He wanted to see the place."

"Welcome, Charlie," Brian said, extending his hand.

They shook, and then Brian said, "We were just heading to the cafeteria. Do you boys want to join?"

"Sure," Eric said.

Charlie nodded. The more time he spent with these guys, the better his chances were at scoring a job down the line.

They took the elevator to the first floor. The cafeteria was huge. It served every kind of food imaginable. There was a pizzeria, a deli, a sushi bar, a tapas counter, and a mobile dessert cart. Plus, everything was free. Charlie had never seen anything like it before.

"I'm going to grab a grilled cheese sandwich," Brian said. "I'll meet you guys at that open table over there once you've gotten your food."

"I'm digging pizza today," said Grayson. "What'll you guys have?"

"There are so many choices," Charlie said.

"Let's try the sushi," Eric interjected. "Come on!"

They parted with Grayson and headed to the sushi bar.

"I would like to order the yellowtail, please, and—"

Somewhere, a cuckoo clock chimed the noontime hour. Then the sound of gunfire rang out like the crackle of fireworks. Charlie and Eric dropped to the floor.

A bearded man with unruly brown hair stood at one end of the cafeteria with an AR-15 semiautomatic assault rifle aimed at the ceiling. He swung the gun around and pulled the trigger in rapid-fire succession. The bullets struck the members of a screaming crowd near the pizzeria—*thwap-thwap-thwap!* Charlie saw Brian Glazier go down in a bloody heap, red goo spouting from a pierced artery in his neck.

Thwap-thwap-thwap!

Now the gun was aimed at the sushi bar. Charlie pulled Eric into the dark shadow of a table. Blood splattered across the floor, and three more bodies fell to the ground, lifeless.

The bearded man shouted, "Nobody move!"

People were sniveling and shaking, trying their best to hide behind counters and under tables.

The gun rattled again, the bullets ricocheting off the walls. There was a collective cry of terror.

"I said, nobody move!" the assailant cried.

The cafeteria went stock-still.

"Today, you are all going to die!" cried the man.

Charlie could see the assailant's legs and feet from under the table. The man was pacing back and forth in front of the elevators. The gun was raised and ready to fire.

Somebody cried out in a shrill voice. "Miles, please! Don't do this!"

Thwap-thwap-thwap!

The shrill voice went silent.

"Nobody gets out of here alive," said the gunman.

Charlie looked at Eric. His friend had pissed his pants and sat trembling in a pool of urine and sweat.

The assailant edged along the wall, his gun still pointed into the crowd. He pushed open the door to the men's room and began firing inside. Screams echoed from inside the bathroom. Then he opened the door to the women's room and let rip another round of gunfire. More screams.

As the gunman fired another round in the direction of the deli, Charlie quickly crawled up to the lifeless body of a woman and pulled a bloody arm over his chest.

"Play dead," Charlie hissed.

Eric caught on and positioned himself on the other side of the woman in a sticky pool of dark blood.

They lay as still as statues as the assailant paced through the cafeteria.

"Please, please!" someone cried.

Thwap-thwap-thwap!

The sound of bullets hitting the tile floor. Then silence.

The gunman walked up a row of long tables, the sound of his footsteps growing nearer. Charlie lay motionless on the ground. He could smell the iron of the woman's blood as it ran freely down his sides and puddled around his shoulder blades. He kept his eyes closed. A shadow passed over him. He could hear the labored breathing of the assailant.

Suddenly, a single shot rang out, and the breathing stopped.

Charlie waited, listening for any sign of movement. When none came, he peeked through a slit in his eyelids and saw the assailant lying dead on the floor with half of his head blown off.

Somebody on the other side of the cafeteria cried out, "It's over! He shot himself!"

* * *

Charlie could hardly keep track of what happened next. A SWAT team dressed head to toe in black flooded the cafeteria, guns raised, crying out for everyone to put their hands in the air. The injured survivors were pulled from the scene. Because they were covered in blood, Charlie and Eric were whisked downstairs to a waiting ambulance to be poked and prodded.

When the paramedics were satisfied that they hadn't suffered any damage, the FBI took down their names and contact information and asked them questions for what seemed like hours. Finally, Charlie and Eric were free to go. The gunman was dead. Eric had learned that Brian Glazier had been pronounced dead at the scene. Grayson McDougal had survived a gunshot to the leg and was undergoing surgery at a nearby hospital.

Eric's driver came to pick them up, and together they drove back to Eric's house. It was already evening when they arrived home. The sun was setting like a golden orb over the blue ocean. Eric and Charlie sat on the patio in silence, not sure what to say.

Finally Eric spoke up. "Thank God you had the idea to play dead. It saved our lives."

Charlie shrugged. All he could think about was the way the gunman had blown his brains out, just like Charles Abernathy Vanderough and Franz Vanderough had done decades before.

CHAPTER 24

THE FOLLOWING WEEK, Charlie penned a letter to Maggie at Helmsley Park:

Dear Maggie,

I had a harrowing experience last week that brought my life into sharp focus. Until now, I could not fully appreciate everything you did for me when I showed up on your doorstep with nowhere else to go. Although we deceived each other, both claiming to be more financially well off than we actually were, I have come to realize that many of my feelings toward you were, nevertheless, true. I did love you in my way. And I know you loved me.

The possibility of us being together is, perhaps, absurd given the circumstances. You have a husband and a child to think of. I am thirty-five years your junior. However,

I would like to extend my hand in friendship—this time under no pretenses. Ron needn't know about our dalliances. I could return to Helmsley House and stay on as your ward. I would be happy to go to work for Ron at the Porsche dealership. Whatever the arrangement, I promise to contribute my fair share to the family earnings, and perhaps together, we can make up for the fortune that Charles Abernathy denied us.

I only hope that you can forgive me. I anxiously await your reply.

—CBV

Over the next several weeks, Charlie received no word from Helmsley Park, and he began to fear that he had permanently severed his connection with the Vanderoughs. Then one hot August day, a letter came for Charlie in the mail. It was from Sonia, the housekeeper:

Dear Charlie,

I received your letter at Helmsley House, and I have spent the better part of the month searching for some trace of Mr. and Mrs. Vanderough and young Ethan so that I may deliver your correspondence to them. I am sorry to report that there has been no sign of them for many weeks now. You see, after you left, Maggie found the pistol under your pillow and threatened to shoot herself in the yard. My father, Abel, wrested the gun from her just in time to save her life. But, alas, he was caught in the crossfire and killed. It was a blow to us all.

After that mournful day, things went downhill for the Vanderoughs. The bank foreclosed on the house, and Ron lost his job at the Porsche dealership. The family was forced to sell all of their belongings at auction and move out. Nobody seems to know where they went or how to contact them. The last I heard, Ron wanted to move to Nantucket, but Maggie said she would prefer Florida. So it is anyone's guess where they ended up.

I have stayed on to look after the old house. I have a mind to buy it back from the bank, as it holds so many memories for me. You see: Abel was not my true father. You were—or rather, Charles Abernathy Vanderough was. Charles and my mother, Ynez, had an affair decades ago, and I am the result of that affair. I know this because Charles Abernathy Vanderough said as much in a letter addressed to me in his will. My adopted father, Abel, never knew of the affair. It would have broken his heart. None of the Vanderoughs knew of the affair, either. I have kept it to myself all these years out of respect for your family and mine.

In his will, Charles Abernathy Vanderough also left me a share of his fortune worth $450,000,000. I have kept this fact a secret until now, as I did not want anyone to connect the dots linking me to my true father. However, now that Abel has died and the Vanderoughs have fled, I am free to do with my fortune as I please. So I think my first step will be to buy Helmsley House for myself.

I was never able to thank Charles Abernathy for this very substantial gift, so I am writing now to thank you, Charlie B. If at all you can remember me, remember me as your child and heir and know that I am grateful.

From the return address on your letter, I see you are in California. Good luck in whatever brings you there. May you have lots of sunshine. I wish you the very best.

Yours Truly,
Sonia Maria Delgado

P.S.: I have enclosed a photograph of my mother, Ynez Mariposa Delgado, per your request.

Charlie removed the photograph from the envelope. There was Charles Abernathy Vanderough standing with his arm around a sturdy Latina woman in a white dress: wide hips, broad shoulders, round brown eyes, soft red lips, and one long dark braid down her back.

AFTERWORD

WITH HIS MEASLY INHERITANCE, Charlie hired an attorney to go after Sonia Maria Delgado. He claimed that Charles Abernathy had not been of sound mind when he had left $450,000,000 in her name. In retaliation, Sonia Maria Delgado hired the best lawyers in the country to get the case thrown out of court.

Charlie stayed on as Eric B's houseguest, eventually securing his own internship at Meta-Haiku. Every day, he would have lunch in the cafeteria where the massacre had occurred, and painful memories of that day would come flooding back.

Charlie B was promoted to associate director of multimedia at Meta-Haiku. He was making a six-figure salary and was beginning to live the life he had envisioned for himself. He hired a driver of his own, put down a mortgage on a house in Mountain View, and acquired a membership to the elite Olympic Club.

Then, shortly after his twenty-fifth birthday, Charlie B stopped going to work. Eric Hsiu could tell Charlie was on the verge of a mental breakdown and suggested Charlie seek professional help. But Charlie refused, dismissing the entire mental-health industry as "hogwash."

In October of 2022, Charlie B jumped off the Bay Bridge.

Charlie B had earned enough money working at Meta-Haiku to commission a clone of his own, to be fashioned one year after his death. That is how I, Charles C Vanderough, came into being. This is the letter Charlie B left for me to read on my eighteenth birthday:

Dear Charlie C,

If you are reading this, then I must be dead. But do not mourn for me. I prefer it this way.

You are the third attempt at something resembling a life. The first Charles screwed up his own life, and then screwed up mine. I'll do my damnedest not to screw up yours.

I leave you everything I own. It isn't much, but it's more than I started out with, and it's enough to get you started.

I implore you: stay away from guns. And bridges. I have a mind to throw myself off every bridge I cross. I don't know if life is even worth living. I'll let you settle that one for yourself.

Best of luck.
Charlie B

A NOTE FROM THE AUTHOR

IF YOU ENJOYED *CUCKOO CUCKOO,* please take the time to visit Amazon.com to rate this book. You have no idea what an author would do for a good review, or even a bad one. It doesn't just help get the word out—it can make an author's day to see what a reader thinks about their work.

If you are interested in joining my author newsletter, in which I announce deals, giveaways, and other noteworthy news, please e-mail info@booleanop.com and request to be added or follow me on Twitter at @NickPonticello.

And check out these other titles by me.

Novels:
Do Not Resuscitate
The Maiden Voyage of the Destiny Unknown

Short Stories:
The Button
Three Wishes: And Other Stories
The Misshapen

ACKNOWLEDGMENTS

THANK YOU to my editors, Carolyn and AK, for catching the little snags that can tank a book. To Re Marzullo for being the first person to read the final cut. To Marlene Okner, who has read more of my writing than anyone in the world and whose encouragement and feedback have made me a better writer. Marlene is one of the most talented writers I have had the privilege of knowing, and I hope you get a chance to read her work one day. To my agent, Stephanie Rostan at LGR Literary, for working tirelessly to get my writing into the hands of the right people so that at least some of it can see the light of day. To the Rockets, without whom I'd have given up long ago. And, finally, to the Monkey—my chosen family. Without you there is no me.

ABOUT THE AUTHOR

NICHOLAS PONTICELLO is an educator and writer in Los Angeles, California. He graduated from University of California, Berkeley, with degrees in mathematics and astrophysics and later earned his master's degree in education from the University of Pennsylvania. Mr. Ponticello is interested in exploring the intersection of science, sustainability, mental health, and education and hopes to encourage more systems thinking and sustainability-themed curricula at the secondary school level.

For more titles by this author, please visit www.booleanop.com.